Noël de Montagnac

Negro Nobodies

Being a series of sketches of peasant life in Jamaica

Noël de Montagnac

Negro Nobodies

Being a series of sketches of peasant life in Jamaica

ISBN/EAN: 9783743408081

Manufactured in Europe, USA, Canada, Australia, Japa

Cover: Foto ©Andreas Hilbeck / pixelio.de

Manufactured and distributed by brebook publishing software (www.brebook.com)

Noël de Montagnac

Negro Nobodies

The . .
Overseas
Library .

NEGRO NOBODIES

NOËL DE MONTAGNAC

NEGRO NOBODIES

Being a Series of Sketches of Peasant Life in Jamaica

LONDON

T. FISHER UNWIN

PATERNOSTER SQUARE

M DCCC XCIX

OVERSEAS LIBRARY

PREFACE

THE DEVIL, some people have a way of saying, is black. A negro, they add, is also black, and then they smile and leave you, a stranger, to come to but one conclusion. This is scarcely fair. For it is plain that even if both be black, a negro is not necessarily a devil. On the contrary, a negro—at least a Jamaica negro —is frequently a man of such excellent character that one is glad to make his acquaintance. More than this, he can be something of a gentleman. The truth is, there are some fine black people in Jamaica, and here is a book concerning them.

Preface

It seems, indeed, scarcely necessary for me to explain the purpose of this book. Jamaica, one of the West Indian Islands, is a British colony—although little sugar is now made in it, there is but one theatre, and the taxes are heavy — and it is interesting to learn something of the people who really belong to it. Also it is interesting to learn the truth about them. Many of these people are the descendants of African slaves, who were not as foolish or faithless as is generally believed ; they are people who, having had few advantages, are yet surprisingly clever with words, who think and feel, and who are certainly not to be despised. They are the people of whom the tourist has been kind enough to write, but of whom he knows nothing ; they are the

Preface

people who have been, and are still, misunderstood. Who, however, more sincerely love their Queen; who, when all things are considered, more truly serve their God? It is such a pleasure to me, therefore, to help to introduce these so-called 'quashies' to those who, more than any others, should always be interested in them, and who should be the first to give the worthy black man the credit that he deserves.

In conclusion, I should like to say that I have purposely given few descriptions of the environment—my business is with the people, not with the scenery — only such descriptions, indeed, as seem to be necessary to make the characters clear. The dialect is very difficult to understand and to write. I trust I have succeeded

Preface

in making it intelligible. What more is there to be said? 'Sutt'nly,' as my friend Zacche, the tailor, has remarked to a customer, 'sutt'nly, sir, there may be faults—whichen no man is perfect, not even a new machine—but I have done my best, and I will thank you kindly to bear that in mind.'

N. DE M.

BOURNEMOUTH,
ENGLAND.

CONTENTS

xi

THE MISTAKE OF SAMUEL UTTOCK

NEGRO NOBODIES

CHAPTER I

THE MISTAKE OF SAMUEL UTTOCK

DIRECTLY Daddy caught a young man trying to hide a girl's Christian name in the folds of a conversation, he knew that they were intimate, and he advised them to marry. 'My son and daughter,' he would say, 'you make haste and married, then you will have plenty time and opportunity to do you' courting. Married, I say, then you becomes respectable persons, and you' conversation is lawful, and you' love is lawful, and every thing about you is thoroughly lawful, and you is really blessëd in de eyes of de Lord.' 'Sutt'nly' (certainly), Zaccheus Mettle, the little pock-pitted tailor, has replied, 'sutt'nly, that's all very well, sounds very well, but what if you married and you finds you make a mistake? Well, sutt'nly, how's that my man, how's that?' To which Daddy gave this answer: 'Zacche, my son, you cut you' cloth and give you'· tongue a rest; this matter is too thick for you' scissors.'

It happened, however, that although Zacche's opinion found favour with many, who were intelligent, Daddy influenced no inconsiderable number. Some of these, it

Negro Nobodies

is only right to say, lived happily ever afterward, but some — 'well,' to use Zacche's words, 'some, sutt'nly, see de devil before they dead.'

The case of Samuel Uttock and Maria Stephens was the worst. Maria begun the courtship. She had seen Sammy slipping down Titchfield Hill, on his way to protect the Reservoir, in a rain that was making a deep sea of the dry land, and, womanlike and logical, she came to the conclusion that if a man could do so much for the mere privilege of being handed a few shillings every Saturday afternoon, he would break his neck for the love of a beautiful woman. Maria was, of course, a beautiful woman. Besides, she had more than once observed that Samuel's suit was made of good

5

material. His studs, she would swear, were gold. From her standpoint, therefore, he was worth having at any cost. Reading, however, in a certain book, entitled *Hints How to be Happy*, that no woman should dream of marrying a man until she had learned how to tickle his palate, Maria questioned Rachel, Samuel's sister, concerning the eccentricities of his taste which affected his stomach. It seemed only to emphasise the suitability of her selection when Maria was informed that a plain dish of red peas and rice, a bit of pear, a roasted plantain and a few sprats fried in cocoanut oil with a little 'bird pepper' would fill Samuel with joy for a fortnight. Maria then made her arrangements.

Samuel had scarcely time to consider

the matter. He knew that Maria loved
him, for she told him so, and he firmly
believed that he loved her also. Once
only, and it was early one Sunday
morning while he was tacking a 'Duke's
Cigarette Cameo' of Ellen Terry as
'Margaret' to the wall of his hut, did
it occur to him that, after all, he might
not really care a button for Maria.
But it was only a thought, and presently he reproached himself for the
ingratitude of it. As soon as it was
convenient, Daddy entertained Samuel
and Maria together at his house, and
painted for them a beautiful picture of
their future life. It would be the
garden of Eden without the devil and
the forbidden fruit. In their enthusiasm
Samuel and Maria kissed each other

several times and swore to be loving
and faithful as long as life lasted.
Before they returned home that evening
the wedding day was fixed, and Daddy
blessed them.

Zacche made the wedding trousers
(the coat and vest, the Inspector's
present, were obtained ready made from
Kingston) but the cutting puzzled him
to such an extent (Sammy being ab-
normally bow-legged) that he declared
the marriage would not turn out well.
'Sutt'nly,' he remarked to me after Sam
had tried on the trousers and pronounced it a misfit, 'sutt'nly, busha,
not every man has such particular bow
legs, and I say that it is not every
tailor can cut to fit that said bow
legs. And, sutt'nly, in de same way

Negro Nobodies

I say that not every woman can fit
de heart of a man with proper legs,
muchen less a man with such extraordinary bow legs.' Sammy was however sanguine, and Maria threatened
to disfigure anyone who had the
temerity to stand between herself and
her adored.

What was considered to be the
honeymoon was spent in a fashion
which convinced both Samuel and Maria
that at least two people could, at a
certain time of their lives, find themselves in a kind of heaven without
dying. Sam gave Maria a Coolie
bangle and three new straw hats; Maria
fed Sam on red peas and rice twice a
day. He filled like the Reservoir and
ran over with joy. Her feelings cannot

be described. In the course of a month, however, Charlie Hooper, a great friend of Zacche's, thought fit to observe, at the termination of a discussion on 'What are the outward and visible signs of Happiness?' that 'what we say we see we don't see,' and that 'single blessedness is, after all, de rightest thing for a poor man.' Then the town opened its eyes to the fact that Sam's affection for Maria was already in a rapid consumption. Indeed, it was dying fast. Sam would hesitate to climb the hill to the hut, and Binn, the fisherman, caught him sitting on the church steps nursing dejection when he should have been at home spooning with Maria.

One afternoon Sam was standing bareheaded with his back to the western door of the church—the door by which he had entered to be married—his chin upon his breast, his hands behind him, having the appearance of a Sambo statue of Chronic Despair. Daddy stole from the vestry and , touched him on the shoulder.

'Sam, my son—' he began.

Uttock faced the beadle, fury flashing from his eyes.

'See here, Missa Daddy,' he hissed, 'see here, sir, mind me and you here this evening. Mind me, old man, I say, mind me. Very well, I give you fair warning and notice.'

'Sam?' But the tone was everything.

The expression on Sam's face immediately changed. His resentment was already in full retreat.

'Ah, my son,' and he smiled in spite of himself, 'you ever see my trial here this blessed Tuesday evening? Old man, what you want? Supposing I was really a bad-tempered man, though?'

There were tears in Daddy's eyes.

'I remember,' said he, speaking softly as if in a dream, 'I remember when I was a young man like you, Sam, and Lucy—ah, Lucy, she was alive then!— Lucy, me and Lucy, we had to bear and forbear, really to bear and forbear, Sam, although Lucy she was such an angel.'

Now Lucy, whom Daddy had married soon after his appointment as beadle of

the church, was said by the town to have
been one of the most noble women that
ever lived. She was so sweet and good
upon all occasions that there were those
even of her own sex who positively
worshipped her. Indeed, it was held that
Daddy had thus been rewarded for his
labours in the Master's vineyard. When
Lucy died the whole town was in tears,
and she must thenceforward be, in its
eyes, a saint. This confession of Daddy's
would, therefore, have been something of·
a revelation to most of the townspeople,
but Uttock failed to appreciate its signifi-
cance. He was, in truth, struck only by
the tenderness of Daddy.

'You is really a kind old man though,
'pon my word,' said Sam ; 'but see
here, Missa Daddy, make we change this

subject. I am well and sore with it already.'

'Well, tell me,' said Daddy, who agreed to change the subject, 'tell me then, my son, what's de said trouble—I mean, boy, how is Maria?'

Daddy's intentions were invariably the best.

'De gal is hell, sa,' exclaimed Sam with spirit. 'Asking you' pardon, Missa Daddy, whichen you is certainly an old man, and a beadle, and we is close de church; but I will speak de truth if—if it be de Judgment Day!'

'Sam, Sam,' said Daddy, 'I fear you is really going down and disappointing de old man.'

'Not so, Missa Daddy,' replied Sam, 'nothing like that. You hear me, sa, 'I did love de gal until I would have drownded myself for her; I did worship her; I make her my idol; I give her a ring; and, certainly, she was a fine gal—except to her nose whichen it has a particular shape that I never did like—well, and you married we. Ah, Missa Daddy, old as you is, beadle though you be, when I think how I tie up, fasten up, *hang* up, in this thing—!'

'Steady, my son,' said Daddy, 'don't harass you'self. Consider de matter; you is married, you have a wife, you is lawful, you—'

'I hear all that before,' broke in Sam, bitterly. 'I hear every bit of that before; and I married this three day gone a month, and I know, and I experience, and I feel, and I can tell you that marriage is a most unlawful thing, being it really mean de utter ruination of two poor people for ever and ever, amen, world without end, amen. Amen.'

'Sam, my son,' said Daddy, on another tack, 'Maria has good qualities, good—'

'But most awfully greedy, sa,' said Sam; 'greedy, sa, and domineering and wanting everything for herself, and with a powerful piece of a temper. Look, I am not a boy, Missa Daddy, and if a man be accustomed to tie his neck-tie in his fashion for the last fifteen year, him is not going to make such a person as a woman tie it for her fashion, whichen is de main cause of de contention. Hi, now, now, now, this gal like sailor knot, I don't like that said kind of sailor knot; then because I does not consent to do as she has a mind, she has an inclination to dig out my eye.'

'I would give up de tie, man,' said Daddy.

'Then she would instantly insist that I make her wear de stud and all de rings — whichen is de second cause of contention. No, Missa Daddy, there is no hope for me now, sa. Lawful or unlawful, proper or improper, I am well and securely married and tied up.'

He carefully removed the perspiration from his face, took breath and continued :

'If I had followed Zacche Mettle, I would have been a free man this day ; but no, what with de soft talking and de devilnation fascination of de gal herself, and *you*, Missa Daddy, I must turn jackass and get married. For what? For her to take a real advantage of me. Now, old man, let me tell you something; this was de said place where I waited for Maria upon de day of de wedding (and I was really happy then, but that is past now), and therefore it is at this said place that I am going to make a vow to done with de gal for ever and ever; she is to go her way, and I am to take my own road for de peace of my soul.'

Daddy had taken a seat on one of the steps of the porch shortly after the conversation commenced, but, when these last words were uttered, he rose quickly, and, with his right hand, covered Sam's mouth.

Negro Nobodies

'Man,' said he sternly, 'in de name of decency, how could you do such a thing?'

'And she will go her way, and I will go my way,' reiterated Sam, like one rightly convinced.

'Sam, my son,' said Daddy, speaking slowly, 'I want you to make me — to make de old man—a promise.'

'Done, Missa Daddy, done,' was Sam's reply. 'There is only one decent thing to do now, and that is to thank you kindly for all you have done. I thank you, old gentleman, for you' good intentions.' Then, suddenly softening his voice, he observed, 'I 'most think there is no more Miss Lucy in this town now.'

Daddy winced.

The Overseas Library

'My son,' said he, with deep emotion, 'whichen you think is more better: you with you' Maria, who is living, or me with my Lucy, who is dead?'

'Well, sa, to tell you de truth, I would much prefer to be you with Miss Lucy.'

'Then,' said Daddy, with fervour, 'you would have a real sorrow and a righteous cause of complaint. You hear me, Sam, thank de Lord, my son, for what you have, greedy and domineering though she be. May be, I say, may be, if Maria died this night, you would come to find she wasn't a bad gal after all.'

CONCERNING A CHRISTENING

CHAPTER II

CONCERNING A CHRISTENING

SPEAKING to me confidentially of the character of Augustus Tilbert, the shipwright, Binn has remarked, ''Gustus, busha, is really a good man, really a man of sense, whichen I told those fellows so the other day, but—' Then, after a pause that meant a good deal, 'You know, sir, his wife has baby again last night?' This was, in truth, Tilbert's one weakness, his certain misfortune of which the town was positively ashamed.

23

Had he too frequently flavoured his 'cool drink' with common rum; had he smoked stale 'donkey rope' tobacco; had he, in building his boats, made it a practice to put putty only in places where oakum and putty should have been; had he, in short, done almost anything but annually increase his family, the town would have felt no embarrassment. It would have regarded the failing in a purely sympathetic light. To have a small family 'was really de privilege of persons whichen have gone to some expense, and trouble, and worry, not to speak of de great responsibility of de thing itself. Besides,' Binn added, 'a family, sir, is necessary and honourable, being it is to prove that de said parties have no ill feelings de one towards de other, nor such a personal thing as a physical disagreement between them. But to have a family of a number is nothing more or less than pure idleness and nonsense — whichen, sir, is a disgrace.' Tilbert himself spoke freely on the subject. 'For a man to have a large family,' he was heard to declare shortly after the birth of his fourth child, 'for a man to be responsible for a whole regiment of pickney — whether it is boy, oh, or gal, oh — he must certainly be very worthless, deceitful and not worthy de consideration muchen less de conversation of decent people. Mark well what I say : now, this is certainly my fourth child, but it is my last child. This make altogether two boys and two gals, whichen I consider is well done and prove everything. So, my friends, I finish with de business. In conclusion, I say I will never be a father again for as long as I live.' The following year, however, he was the father of twins.

When, about a week after I arrived in Port Antonio, I became acquainted with Tilbert and his wife, there was fair promise of the ninth child. Tilbert was thin and evidently much distressed, and he hesitated somewhat to commence a sentence; while his wife wore the expression of a woman who, having been constantly confused, could form no accurate idea of what was likely to happen. Indeed, the trouble had so far affected Tilbert that he began to imagine foolish things. He told me, for example, that he was certain some wretched person (who probably envied his success with boats) had bargained with an evil spirit to work his ruin. The bargain would be made, of course, by means of an obeah man. It was curious how the evil spirit worked. Tilbert was made to feel that he would not see heaven unless he kept on fathering babies. For a number of years, he further told me, with tears in his eyes, he was firmly of the opinion that he would be responsible for only a small family — 'whichen as you know, busha, is nothing contrary or improper,' but now he felt as if his family would keep on increasing in an extraordinary manner until he died. As he was still, properly speaking, a young man, and as he was endeavouring to live long, he might be responsible for forty children. Then, what would he do with them?

The Overseas Library

The mere idea of being the father of forty children gave him a cough, and made him perspire until his knees trembled. At nights he could no more sleep than fly. What was he to say? What, indeed, was he to do?

When that ninth child was·born, Tilbert called at my house late in the evening to tell me that he had determined to drown himself. Hanging was unsafe, he said. In such an extreme case it would have been unwise for me to speak lightly, so I frowned, and vowed to him that if ever he attempted to do such a thing, I should have him imprisoned where he would be deprived of his cool drink for a month. The town was a good deal more severe. Binn, the 'boss' or chief fisherman, representing the married men,

Negro Nobodies

and Hooper and 'Needlecase' Phillips, the shoemaker, representing the unmarried men, arrested Tilbert on his way to work the following morning to ask him whether he did not think he had already sufficiently disgraced them all, and especially whether, in view of this last offence, he did not think he merited some sort of punishment. Hooper, clearing his throat, suggested that Tilbert should be shipped to Hayti or Colon 'for a time.' Tilbert, however, preferred to remain where he was. Hayti, he informed them, was rather hot just then, and Colon was always deadly damp. There was only one man in Port Antonio who seemed thoroughly to appreciate the painfulness of poor Tilbert's position, and from whom, therefore, Tilbert could expect genuine sympathy. He was Daddy.

Daddy not only entertained a sincere
affection for Tilbert, and provided him
many a day with the means of obtaining
the wholesome bread to eat which was,
after all, better than any kind of cheap
ginger and water and sugar—that 'cool
drink' of which he was so fond—but
Daddy had ever a kind word for Rosa,
Tilbert's wife, and he evinced a substantial
interest in the children, beginning with
Arthur Augustus. When the *Phantom*,
the yacht which Tilbert built, won the
Governor's cup at the Regatta in Kingston, was it not Daddy who backed his
congratulations by five shillings and a
black coat, the material alone of which
was, according to Zacche, worth half-a-
sovereign? Also when Clarentina Maud
Jane Franseca, another of Tilbert's chil-

dren, had the cough that Mother Bet declared was 'consumption's first cousin,' was it not Daddy who supplied the nourishment and whó helped to save her life? Ay, there was no friend like Daddy.

In Tilbert's present trouble Daddy again showed the strength of his affection. Instead of swelling the unison of uncharitable criticism on the conduct of the unfortunate shipwright, he must apologise for the whole business, and take infinite pains to convince the unbelieving that that ninth child would be Tilbert's last. Daddy, in short, pacified the town.

Late in the afternoon previous to the christening I found Tilbert standing at the bench 'rubbing up' a firmer chisel and two plane irons. Phillips seemed to be ˙ propping the meagre cocoanut shed under which a skiff was being timbered. Scott and Burnet were leaning on the old galley (Tilbert's tool store), and Binn reclined in his large seine canoe. Zacche, who could not be comfortable unless his feet were touching the ground, was seated on an oil drum. Behind them Arthur and a little girl were collecting shavings. Hooper followed me closely, and as he came up to him, he slapped Tilbert on the shoulder, saying:

'Hi, man, I hear you take this last pickney and make nine you' grand total. Hi, yes, for true, no nonsense this time. And you going to stop introducing pickney to us all. Hi, yes,' addressing Scott and Burnet, ''Gustus really has that intention. He has done well, and he conclude to draw out de business.'

Negro Nobodies

Now, Tilbert had a temper.

'Well, and what's that to you?' said he sharply. 'De devil take de whole of you all—asking you' pardon, busha, for de said expression—you is well ignorant and interfering and forward. Supposing I even choose to have *forty* children' (here, however, he shivered), 'and supposing I choose to have *none*, what is it to you all, I say?'

'Hi, but you can't choose to have none,' rejoined Hooper quietly, 'only because, of course, you have nine already. Hi, yes, you mustn't be vexed, for that's de truth what I am telling you now.'

'Done, done!' exclaimed Burnet, a lover of peace, 'done, Charlie. Cho, man, you ought to know better than to continue to harass 'Gustus in such a manner. You

c

think it is boy business this? You think it is play play for one single man to have nine living pickney in seven year?'

'Well, we not saying nothing to that,' drawled Hooper. 'All we saying is, that 'Gustus not going to bother to have any more baby again.'

'Well, sutt'nly, gentlemen,' said Zacche, springing to his feet, 'there should be no contention in this matter. Sutt'nly, if a man is idle enough to get married— whichen is to hang himself, don't forget that—as a rule he will have babies. Just de same as if you drink thick split peas' soup upon an empty stomach, in nine cases out of every ten you will have a spasm. De one thing follows de other. And, sutt'nly, de more baby, de more de poor man must miserable—that is, if a poor man can be any more miserable after his wedding day. But, howsomever, that's not de point I have in my mind. Sutt'nly Missa Daddy tell me that to-morrow morning (please God, no damage!) 'Gustus's last boy pickney is to have a christening. Now, sutt'nly, all I want to know is what name 'Gustus is determined to call that said boy pickney.'

''Gustus,' said Binn from the bottom of the canoe, 'you give de baby name yet?'

'Well, to tell you de truth,' Tilbert replied, 'I don't decided yet. De fact is, by this time I almost use up all de name I can think upon. Howsomever, as it is a boy, Rosa want to give him name just so-so Willie. Willie, nothing more. *Willie Tilbert*, and I think I will agree to that.'

'Hi, but how can you do such a thing?'

said Binn, sitting bolt upright. 'In de first place, de name is too short, whichen it is almost indecent, and in de second place, one of you' pickney has de said name in de middle of two others already, whichen you should know.'

'Hi, and in de third place, de sweetness of de name Willie, Willie, Willie all day long is going to induce 'Gustus to bother with baby again.'

But as this remark of Hooper's was considered irrelevant, no one noticed it.

'Well, sutt'nly,' said Zacche, who it could be seen was itching to make a speech, 'sutt'nly there is no such name as Willie. Sutt'nly there is a name, *William*, whichen Willie is de short of, and so, sutt'nly, without William you cannot have Willie. A short name make out of a long name, and a nickname generally make out of itself, being it has a double especial particular meaning. For example, sutt'nly Missa Daddy real name is Daniel Rutherford, whichen is well known, but Daniel is connected with de Scriptures, whichen is holy and sacred, and Rutherford is a great trouble to a poor man jaw bone, more so if you don't take time how you call it, by which means we all consent to say Missa Daddy. Then there is Hellick. Sutt'nly if his mother was alive this day she would kill any person for having an idea that she could call her one boy pickney so-so Hellick. Well, no, sutt'nly his name is Alexander James Macfarlane Binn. Then there is John Scott, him we call Scotty. Charles Stapleton Hooper, he is Charlie—'

'Hi, and Zaccheus Belinfante Mettle,' yawned Hooper, under the bench, 'he is Zacche.'

'Well, sutt'nly,' pursued Zacche, 'these are example of long name that is made short name. Towards de nickname, then, we have "Needlecase." By rights (whichen we have heard Mother Bet, his godmother, say) Needlecase proper name is Abraham Nathaniel Phillips. Being, however, he has such a long length— and I must know, for I measure him—and being he really favour de said insect (whichen I am paying him a compliment), we call him Needlecase. Well, sutt'nly, it's not his fault if he has a likeness to a needlecase or a grasshopper.'

'Anyhow,' observed Phillips, who had deliberately turned his back upon Zacche, 'anyhow I would sooner be a needlecase than such a thing as a beetle. I would sooner see everything that is to be seen from de elevation of six feet than see nothing, and feel lonesome and most cold and miserable from de level of four.'

'Well,' said Binn, 'all what Zacche say is true. De name *Willie* don't fascinate me at all, whichen I have said before, so I think 'Gustus better make an elevation to get another name.'

'That is it,' Tilbert answered. 'I am really sorry, Alexander Binn, that I don't please you, whichen I will thank you kindly if *you* could give me a name.'

'Well, sutt'nly, take Jeroboam,' suggested Zacche.

'Nothing of de kind,' said Burnet instantly, 'for that is de name of Inspecta

Gresham bull dog, whichen is de terror and de sorrow of de place.'

'Well,' said Scott, who sometimes stammered, 'gi-give him name Na-Na-Na-Na Na—'

'Hi, but what a beautiful new name that is!' observed Hooper.

'See here,' said Burnet encouragingly, 'you don't mind Charlie. You take time, Scotty, my brother. We will wait upon you.'

'Napoleon,' said Scott, and he sat down.

'You, sir,' said Binn, almost savagely, 'don't you ever talk so lightly upon such a terrible, powerful, royal, foreign name as that!'

'See here, then, how is Reginald?' asked Needlecase.

'Very good indeed, really first class,' replied Tilbert. 'Both me and Rosa really take a great fancy to de said name, but de misfortune is we make use of it already.'

'Well, sutt'nly, I have it,' said Zacche. 'Call that particular boy pickney — er — Constantine.'

Scott and Burnet opened their mouths and then nodded approval, but Tilbert must be guided by Binn.

'What you think of that name, Hellick?'

'Well, 'Gustus,' said Binn, 'being I am really to give you my opinion, I am saying that foreign names, like foreign victuals, don't suit us poor Jamaica black people. De truth is, I much prefer one of our old time common name.'

'Well, then,' said Scott, who was

commencing to fidget, '*you* give us a name.'

'Johnson,' said Binn decisively, '*Johnson Tilbert*. Now, that is a suitable name if you like.'

To this assertion there was but one reply, and it came from Hooper, who, it seemed, had just awakened from a doze.

'Hi, you is all getting on first class,' said he, 'first class and number one with name for 'Gustus last pickney, but de only thing is, of course, you don't quite hit upon de rightest one yet ; and, of course, you didn't want to disturb my rest to ask for my opinion too — that I know. Hi, yes, I thank you kindly for you' great consideration and all that.'

Negro Nobodies

Tilbert looked very unhappy. He tried to say something, but failed, and Hooper, evidently taking compassion, softened his voice and said:

'Well, make we call him, *Nebber-could-a-make-a-razor*' (Nebuchadnezzar). 'Hi, yes, I am not making a piece of a joke; I mean what I say, of course. "Nebber-could-a-mek-a-razor" was de name of a king; and, if de pickney live, it will proud of it. Besides, de name will always remind 'Gustus not to bother with any more baby again.'

But this suggestion of Hooper's carried no weight, and Tilbert hurried home to tell Rosa that it was likely the child would be baptised without a name.

The following morning was bleak, misty, muddy and forbidding; nevertheless, from an early hour Daddy was about, on Tilbert's behalf, inviting people to the christening. Binn was then upon the sea superintending his men at work with the seine; nor could Scott attend, for, rivalling Hooper as Jack-of-all-trades, he had, he said, to pick a cart-load of cocoanuts, whitewash a hut, make a coffin, dress and bury an old acquaintance, cook and eat his dinner, and make a tray of peppermint sugar candy before sunset. But Phillips, Uttock and several others accepted the invitation. Consequently there was a fairly large gathering in the church at eight o'clock when the service commenced. Hooper and Zacche having, for a reason which is to appear, consented to be the godfathers, were among the most conspicuous. A fat - faced,

Negro Nobodies

heavy girl, named Verona Machonochie
—Rosa's bosom friend—and Rosa herself were the godmothers.

Now this was a service that many had
cause to remember. It commenced in
the usual manner, but, just as the Gospel
was about to be read, Hooper was
seized by a fit of coughing, the effect,
he whispered to Zacche, of the rather
damp draught in which he was standing,
and which affected him, of course, because he was thinner and more delicate
and spiritual than either Zacche or 'de
two gal them,' meaning Rosa and Verona, the godmothers. This remark was,
nevertheless, loud enough to be heard,
and several people smiled, including the
minister, Mr Blackburn. Indeed, in order
that he might continue to conduct the

service with dignity, he must keep his eyes upon the prayer-book. The Gospel was then read, and the service proceeded. The minister now addressed the godfathers and the godmothers.

'Dost thou, in the name of this child, renounce the devil and all his works, the vain pomp and glory of the world, with all covetous desires of the same, and the carnal desires of the flesh, so that thou wilt not follow nor be led by them?'

'Well, sutt'nly we do, we do, we do,' said Zacche, in a loud, business - like voice.

Someone burst out laughing, he could not help doing so, and Mr Blackburn did not raise his head for a second or two.

'No, my good man,' said he, striving

not to smile, 'you must not answer like that. You must wait a little, and I will tell you what to say. Now, repeat after me, "I renounce them all."'

'Hi, yes,' observed Hooper, 'that's what we mean; only, of course, Zacche was a little too quick for you.'

I thought Daddy would have fallen.

'Wilt thou be baptised in this faith?' continued the minister.

For a few seconds no one spoke, then Hooper, seeing that Zacche was framing an answer, pulled him to one side, saying :

'That is for de gal them to answer. Hi, yes. We answer for our part done already.'

Mr Blackburn, however, kept his countenance.

The Overseas Library

'Name this child,' said he presently.

Here Tilbert, greatly embarrassed, looked at Daddy. Daddy whispered to Rosa, who shook her head and sighed. Meanwhile Hooper was helping Zacche to pull from a pocket a long slip of paper which was handed to the minister.

'Is this the name of the child?' he asked.

'Well, suttn'ly, sir, it is,' Zacche replied.

'It's rather a long name,' said the minister. 'What is it? Simon, Peter, Mount—what's this?—Mount S—oh, Mount Sinai. *Simon, Peter, Mount Sinai Tilbert.*'

Hooper smiled, Tilbert started and the baby screamed.

'Is that to be the name of your child? said Mr Blackburn, addressing Tilbert.

'Well, rector,' replied the shipwright,

Negro Nobodies

'I suppose it is, whichen it is a decent name, I think, and so I really thank Zacche for de mention of it.'

'Simon, Peter, Mount Sinai?' said Mr Blackburn. '*Simon Peter* is all right enough; but, my good man, *Mount Sinai* is the name of a mountain.'

'Hi, yes, well, we all know that,' said Hooper dryly; 'but it is going to be de name of 'Gustus last boy pickney from this day. *Simon* we give him name for his father sake; *Peter* we give him name for his mother sake; *Mount Sinai* we give him name for our sake; *Mount* is for Zacche, and *Sinai* is for me. Hi, yes! This is de last of de name them. De name, in this quarter, for pickney all done, and, of course, 'Gustus done with de name them.'

'Well, sutt'nly, excuse me, sir,' said Zacche, stepping nearer to the minister, *Simon, Peter, Mount Sinai Tilbert*, is de said name whichen we have given unto you for this said boy pickney, and so, sutt'nly, sir, you can proceed.'

And the child was christened.

ELIZABETH WALTERS DIS-
COVERS A DUPPY

CHAPTER III

I T was after six o'clock on a Friday evening, in the still, warm, feeble twilight to which, in this part of the world, we are accustomed, that Letitia Burke, who occupied a hut half way up Richmond Hill, stopped grating cassava to listen to screams out - screaming one another somewhere near the old church and the tall cocoanut tree on the top of that hill. Her first and altogether natural impression was that a certain wicked one

53

of the dead, having stepped out of his tomb at the instigation of a powerful obeahman in the parish, was making the noise, was signalling, in fact, according to a perfectly understood and diabolical plan. But when the screams were presently succeeded by healthy cries for help, in a voice which she recognised, Letitia hurried to Binn's house, which was close by, to ask him what he intended to do. Binn had a habit of considering a case in two or three respects before he consented to take it up—a habit which may or may not have been fostered by laziness—and he therefore told Letitia to sit and to keep quiet for a few minutes while he looked carefully into the matter. Before, however, he was able to determine on a course of action, Charlie Hooper was seen

conducting to her house, in a distressed
condition, the unfortunate subject of the
disturbance, Elizabeth Walters, an inoffen-
sive young woman, who supported herself
and her two children by sweeping the
church, washing clothes and selling
poultry. Hooper must have found her
in the graveyard, for they were walking
from that direction. Several people now
beset Elizabeth, and put questions to
which she paid little attention. Hooper
did not seem much concerned; naturally,
for he was at the bottom of the whole
business. There were sympathisers enough,
however, Rachel Uttock, Samuel's sister,
being the loudest. When her hut was
reached, Elizabeth heaved a sigh of relief,
and became sufficiently communicative to
say that, searching the graveyard to find

a missing hen and two chickens, she had seen a duppy. The women could not believe their ears. They must tremble. Another terrible ghost had come to light. Who could now face the graveyard even in the glare of the unclouded noon? The Lord only knew what would happen next. The world was undoubtedly coming to an end. At all events, Elizabeth had seen something and had suffered; some one had put obeah on her, said they, and it was 'really a shameful piece of wickedness,' Rachel remarked, 'considering de poor gal has no husband and de two pickney them is so awfully young.' Binn called at about nine o'clock to say that, after carefully considering the matter, he had come to the conclusion that the duppy, who must have been a splendid judge of fowls, had taken the hen and the two chickens; and that, as they were worth having and the duppy must have been hungry, he would on no account give them up. Some of the neighbours, however, thought that it would be wise and seemly to propitiate that duppy; wherefore rum was bought and handed round, and a few hymns, including the old hundredth, were sung for this purpose. Indeed it was but an excuse for 'a little excitement and such like,' that led to a 'scene' which, had it been possible, would have annoyed even a broad-minded duppy.

On the following morning, a Saturday, which was observed as a kind of holiday, Zacche opened his shop to accommodate a portion of the town who had gathered to discuss the duppy. In respect to his position as beadle, Daddy was asked to take the chair; which was, actually, to sit on the table. Zacche then stood on a soap box beside him, and made a short, pertinent speech, in which he said that, certainly, the whole thing — meaning the occurrence of the previous evening—was 'pure foolishness and monkey business from first to last;' and that he encouraged them to occupy his shop for the purpose of discussing the matter only because he would avail himself of the opportunity to show them a coat, fine in material, fashionable in style and comfortable to wear, which he had finished. After exhibiting the coat and receiving two orders (the customers, however, providing their own material), Zacche made room for Binn to open the discussion.

Negro Nobodies

'Well, my friends,' began Binn deliberately, 'I have no book learning, only de one sense God Almighty give me, but I say that if there is no duppy upon Richmond Hill, then my grandmother—whichen she is now dead and taking her rest, I hope, poor old lady—my grandmother, gentlemen, is a herring.'

'Of course there is duppy,' said Scott, who was carefully seated in a corner on an old three-legged stool, 'there is duppy certainly. If there was no duppy about de place, then person wouldn't take into them head suddenly to die, more especially at night time. And I must know, for nearly de whole of my family dead in this fashion.'

'And my poopa' (father) 'and cousin too,' said a boy, who had been listening attentively. 'De. blow de duppy give my cousin Tommy knock out de whole of his front teeth them.'

'Well, sutt'nly, my son,' observed Zacche, 'that may have been from a fall.'

Two women and Burnet, the dog-catcher, now boisterously tackled this side issue, but, Daddy rebuking them, they became silent.

'And sutt'nly,' pursued Zacche, 'it's not only a duppy can knock out de whole of a man's front teeth, make me tell you that. Howsomever, to go back to de particular point, I say, sutt'nly, there is no such thing as a duppy or spirit or ghost or rolling calf, and so on. A person which has no substance is not a person at all, and cannot exist.' And Zacche sat down.

Negro Nobodies

'Hear what Missa Daddy say,' and 'We is waiting for Missa Daddy' were now the expressions of the few present who found it difficult to express themselves.

'My dear brethren,' said Daddy, after the fashion of the minister, 'de blessed Scriptures, to which we look for light in all these matters of de other world —de sacred Scriptures, my dear brethren, is not very clear upon de point, therefore I can tell you nothing. Certainly, Mr Blackburn has told me privately that there are no duppies, as we call them, but that *spirits*, my beloved brethren, good and evil spirits, may or may not exist. I think, after all, it is a question of eyesight.'

'Of eyesight and all other sight, no

doubt,' said Tilbert, imitating Daddy. 'Some people, my beloved sisters and brothers, see with four eyes and hear with four ears. That is de reason why —asking you all pardon for leaving de point a little — that is de great reason why some people know more of a person's private affairs than de said person know himself or herself, whichen we all can prove. But howsomever and neverthe-less, I am agreeing with you, Missa Daddy, that there may or may not be duppy. Hellick Binn is a ripe man, and he says there is. Zacche Mettle — whichen, we are proud to say, have a great sense, although he is little in statues —he says there is not. Most of us is with Binn, because we *see* duppy and *feel* duppy. Anyhow, my beloved sisters and brothers, it is a terrible, terrible thing to think upon.'

'What did 'Lizbeth see, though?' said someone, suddenly.

Elizabeth was there to answer in person. She had joined the company with the hope of enlisting substantial sympathy for the loss of her poultry. Wiping her eyes, this is what Elizabeth said :

'At about six o'clock last night — whichen Rachel Uttock know is de said time I am accustomed to pen up my fowl them — I missed two of my white cock chickens and a trash - coloured hen which give me an egg every day without missing. I had no idea where they took themself, but I make up my mind to look in de graveyard where fowl has been found. I look, and look, and look, and see nothing. Presently though, I think I see one of de cock chickens picking a blade of grass close poor old Missa Jorden grave, and so I stooped to catch it. Well, sir, as I could turn to get up (being it was not de said chicken) I saw a person — oh, Lord, such a most outrageous person! He was wearing a long white frock with plenty of red spots upon it, and he had one large red eye and not a single sign of a nose — my good Missa Daddy, de most ugliest, awfullest thing I have ever seen in my life. Well, sa, de person —whichen, as I have said, it was a male—moved his arms so and so' (putting her arms into a circular motion) 'as if he did really have de intention of hugging me up. And, Lord!, my sweet brothers and sisters, upon de mere thought of such a thing, my head just turn round and round and round, and I knew nothing more. Then I wake up all of a sudden to feel Charlie Hooper and another young man, greatly favouring Missa Mettle, pinching me, and Missa Hooper kept on saying, "Miss 'Lizbeth, Miss 'Lizbeth, get up, get up; don't die for de sake of a so-so cock chicken."'

She paused, on the advice of Rachel, to calm herself, and Zacche seized the opportunity to remark that certainly the ways of women were the most mysterious. Binn then rose and pointed out with dignity that, as a matter of fact, the ways of duppies, and not the ways of women, were the most mysterious. To

E   65

which Zacche, who was a little excited, replied :

'So you say, my man, so you say; but you have got to prove, sutt'nly, as I said before, that there is such a thing as a duppy at all. What is a duppy, Hellick Binn? Answer me that. Sutt'nly, I have walked about a great deal and in de darkness of de night, and I never see a duppy from I born.'

'No contention, brethren, no contention,' Daddy called out. 'Maybe *Charlie* has something to say?'

Charlie, as a matter of fact, was dozing, but, hearing his name so distinctly called, he opened his eyes and asked quietly whether they had all finished speaking. They had not, they said. So he shut his eyes again.

66

Negro Nobodies

'De point is, gentlemen,' said a little smooth - faced fisherman, who had not spoken before, 'de point is that whether there is duppy oh, or whether there is no duppy oh, a great calamity has be-fallen this gal, 'Lizbeth Walters, with her two young pickney them, who has lost her hen and her two good cock chickens.' Then, seeming to think that he had made a fool of himself, he disappeared.

It was, however, a sensible observa-tion, and much appreciated; so Daddy proposed, seconded by Binn, that a sum, representing the value of the lost poultry, should be collected and handed to Elizabeth. The proposition was unanimously carried; indeed, a por-tion of the amount, two shillings, I think, was subscribed then and there and given to Elizabeth, who left the shop in excellent spirits.

The discussion revived.

'Zaccheus Mettle,' said Binn, facing the tailor, 'you mean to tell me that that gal—whichen she is well intelligent—did not see a duppy upon Richmond Hill, in de graveyard, last night?'

'Sutt'nly, no,' instantly replied Zacche, 'because, Alexander Binn, there was no such thing as a duppy for 'Lizbeth to see—whichen I have said before.'

'A duppy box *myself* 'pon Richmond Hill last year,' observed Scott parenthetically, and in what he deemed an undertone.

'You hear that, Zaccheus Mettle?' exclaimed Binn, striking the soap box. 'Scotty and all see duppy upon Richmond Hill. Cho, man, confess you is wrong. Behave you'self, I say!' .

'Duppy is there. Duppy is there, my son,' hysterically muttered three-fourths of the company. 'Duppy 'pon Richmond Hill, in de graveyard, to-day, to-day. There's a thing, oh, Lord!'

'Zacche, man,' said Tilbert cautiously, 'you think they are tying you up? I can't see you at all.'

'Sutt'nly,' replied Zacche boldly, but a little like a parrot, 'free speech is de birthright of every gentleman. There-fore, gentlemen, say what you like. See you' duppy, make you' duppy, cook you' duppy, *eat* you' duppy; but de day I ever catch Charlie Hooper—'

'Eh, what's matter? You all done?' and, sitting up, Hooper yawned.

The Overseas Library

For a few seconds no one spoke. Binn's coal - black face, which always shone, now shone more than ever.

'Speak then, my son,' pleaded Daddy, who was fidgeting, 'relieve you' mind; speak.'

'Charlie Hooper,' said Tilbert and two others together, in solemn tones, 'Charlie Hooper, man, Charlie, does you know anything concerning this great and wonderful affair?'

'If I know anything,' said Hooper, clearing his throat, 'If I know anything? Well, I was only de ghost. I don't know if that is anything. And, what is more, I could tell you that all this time. Hi, yes! Let me see now. I remember I buy a gill clay pipe and I dress myself (I am sorry de young lady

did not think me a handsome fellow)
and I qualify for a duppy for a short
while. Zacche (you see I am telling
you everything), Zacche was my assistant, hi, yes, but, as usual, he was a
little late, and so I get no assistance
at all, only he did oblige de gal with a
measure of consolation upon de spot, by
giving her a couple pinch them to wake
her up, for she was sleeping too soon.
Now, that is all. Hi, ladies and gentlemen, you look surprised!'

'But now, now, now, sa,' said Binn,
who had recovered his composure, 'what
in this world ever possessed this big,
ripe man to do such a thing?'

'Idleness, pure idleness and mischief,
and nothing better to do with himself,'
said someone quickly.

'And love of fowl too,' said another, in a light voice.

'Well,' said Hooper, 'I don't deny that. And, of course, *I* am de only one who like fowl. But, being I am de means of giving a lonesome gal a subscription, and being the hen and de two cock chicken is roosting under de gal bed at this minute, I think I should get a subscription too for my generosity and all that. Howsomever, I will make you all a present of it. Hi, yes, I am not joking! And, don't forget, I did also want to feel how duppy feel. Hi, yes, duppy is a nice thing man, more so if he could always manage to give de gal them a little harmless hugging up for old time sake and all that. Hi, yes! Now you see I give you a lot of news, and I don't charge for it, so you must look out to thank me—when you see me another time.' And, smiling, he went his way.

But the people, whose superstitions had been thus nourished, as you might say, still believed that Elizabeth had seen a duppy on Richmond Hill, and none of them ventured near the place for a long time afterwards.

'REST AND BE THANKFUL'

CHAPTER IV

THE cottage in which Daddy lived stood in a decent place on the east side of Titchfield Hill. Two years before his marriage, acting on Lucy's advice, he drew from the Savings Bank the creditable sum which luck with June fish had enabled him to save, and purchased the premises, the house being then in considerable disrepair. There were only two people—the minister and Mr Petlock, of the Public Works Department—to con-

77

gratulate Daddy on the good sense displayed by this transaction; the majority, who knew best (as is usually the case) thought that he might just as well have thrown his money into the sea. Later on, however, when, according to Daddy's own plans, the cottage took a new shape, and became, to some extent, a handsome dwelling, the majority stammered that he had been wiser than them all.

From any corner of the cottage the view was pleasing, but it was perhaps from Daddy's bedroom window that you obtained the finest sight. Standing there, your eye caught a bit of the slender, naked lighthouse, followed distinctly three-fourths of the dark mangrove belt, which the billows loudly beat, and rested on

Negro Nobodies

the beautiful eastern basin, on the broad, placid rim of which many kingly cocoanut trees placed the shadows of their crowns. In the fierce, sweating sunlight, the colours of the limbs of the cocoanut and the leaves of the other trees, and of the water and the sky, were gorgeous gold and green and blue—that blue which is very blue. On a clear, moonlight night the bit of lighthouse winked a watery eye, and the belt seemed to mysteriously broaden. Then the limbs of the cocoanut trees appeared more grey than green, and they were feathery. Over the silvered surface of the basin, through a kind of silken mist, the north wind raised little ripples, and sometimes blew a sail. These two pictures—the one the oil painting, so to speak, the other the steel engraving—Daddy had in mind when he bought the cottage, for the beadle was by nature an artist.

In addition to the house, there was a piece of land of an appreciable size, which Daddy divided into a flower and vegetable garden. In the former, after a time, the bed of violets was something to see. The vegetables, however, did not turn out well. Many of the cabbage, for example, 'sutt'nly,' as Zacche expressed it, 'never did favour cabbage at all.' The tomatoes greatly lacked flavour, and the peppers 'sutt'nly they was either too hot or not hot enough; but,' added Zacche, 'sutt'nly not only beadle pepper have that particular contraryness.' Besides the vegetables, there were a few fruit trees, namely, a yam mango, starapple,

naseberry and several banana. Daddy
watered the yam mango especially,
because he believed in it. A good yam
mango, he held, was nourishment — for
a beadle at any rate. Bananas, on the
other hand, unless eaten with bread, pro-
moted spasms, which might be fatal.
He considered, however, that banana
fritters, properly sprinkled with brown
sugar, were not only delicious but
strengthening. And, said he, they agreed
with old people. Both gardens were pro-
tected from the frivolity of neighbouring
poultry, chiefly chickens, by two neat
white - washed fences that met a grey
gate, close to the front steps, on the
top of which was painted in small, uneven, black letters, the name of the
cottage—'Rest and be thankful.'

The Overseas Library

The house, thatched, plastered and white-washed, was entirely weather proof. It consisted of four rooms, which were also washed as frequently as was necessary to make them look clean. The largest was Daddy's bedroom. It contained, principally, a wide, heavy, mahogany bedstead that could have held four, stout, quiet sleepers, or one little child that sleeps not, but cries and rolls and kicks. Daddy, for as many years as he was able, varnished this bedstead every Queen's birthday. He could not bear a mark upon it. Room number two was the children's, but, after Lucy's death, when Michael and Mary were able properly to dress and undress themselves, it became Mary's, Michael sleeping with his father. Mary made it the

sweetest room in the house. Above the
head of the bed were pasted two finely-
executed plates, one 'Mary and Martha,'
and the other 'The Resurrection.' To
the right and left of these were tacked
illuminated texts also from the Scriptures,
the largest being, 'I am that bread of
life. John vi. 48.' On one of the walls
were gummed prints, from the *Illustrated
London News*, of the Earl of Beaconsfield,
the Right Hon. W. E. Gladstone, Mr
Parnell, the Queen, the Prince of Wales,
the Duke of Cambridge and an old lady,
no doubt a distinguished philanthropist,
whose name had been inadvertently removed. Below these, torn and a trifle
out of line, stuck coloured plates of
'The Latest Spring Fashions,' from the
Young Ladies' Journal. Through the

little window, when the day was done, the sweet, delicate, tamarind-leaf jasmine, which Mary cared, would breathe into the room.

In the smaller of the two other apartments, on a plain, deal board table, the simple fare of the family was nevertheless respectably placed at the proper times. The brick-coloured water jug or 'monkey' was ingeniously balanced on a mahogany chair having a seat two inches thick, but only one leg. The family sat on a bench. If there was a friend to dinner, Michael waited until he had finished, or sat with the tin plate in his lap, on the doorstep. The safe, marked A B & Co., in which straw hats had been packed to Port Antonio, was supported by four legs, which stood in

Negro Nobodies

as many fresh salmon tins filled with kerosene oil and water, to disappoint ants. In the larger apartment, the family received visitors. As you entered it, your eyes fell on the strong mahogany sideboard (which was also varnished on the twenty-fourth of May), and the large, heavy, curiously - shaped tumblers, decanters, wine-glasses, and the odd cups and saucers upon it. These were chiefly ornamental. The few tumblers appropriated for the use of distinguished visitors were put in a corner by themselves. The family, and friends like Binn and Zacche, used pans. There was only one table, and it was covered with a bit of sail cloth. On it were placed a lamp like a lighthouse (something to be proud of), and several books — the

The Overseas Library

Bible, *Pilgrim's Progress*, a Walker's dictionary, an *Inquire within for Everything*, and some others. But there were three or four chairs, a cane seat among them, the largest of which, an arm chair, was proffered the minister when he called. On entering, the visitor scraped the mud from his feet on to a yard or so of coarse, cocoanut matting. Then, by request, he laid his hat and umbrella on the table and sat down. All which emphasised the respectability and fine taste of the beadle. I know, as a matter of fact, that he was proud of the cottage, and that he strove to keep it the neatest of its size on the hill.

I fancy I have climbed from the town and followed the stony carriage road to the corner, where it turns west to the little hotel, and that, standing at this corner, I see the verdant crowns of the cocoanut trees; the dark, thatched roof; the white walls; Mary's window, with the sweet tamarind-leaf jasmine framing it; the banana, with their broad leaves and heavy hands propped near the window; the yam mango, green and trim, beside the banana; the starapple; the red hibiscus; the fence; the grey gate and the name, uneven but distinct, 'Rest and be thankful.'

MICHAEL AND MARY

CHAPTER V

WHEN first I saw Michael he was standing in the sun, sweating from every pore, with his back to a banana tree. I recognised him instantly. He was taller, broader and more finely figured than his father, but his features were unmistakably Daddy's. When he learnt who I was he insisted that I should have the minister's chair, and kindly offered to call his father, who was at the beach calking a canoe. But I said I had no intention of disturbing Daddy, and that I would wait until he returned.

The Overseas Library

Michael would then have resumed work, but I opened a conversation with him, from which I gathered many interesting facts having reference especially to the days of his childhood.

Michael was four years old when his mother died. Consequently, you may say, he never knew her. For a long time he believed his aunt Matilda (Lucy's sister, who was stout and bad-tempered) was his mother. It affected his growth. One Sunday evening, however, when he suddenly realised that she was only his aunt, he immediately hid himself behind a box, he said, and thanked God from the bottom of his heart. And he began to grow from the following morning. At school Michael was considered amiable, but a fool. Indeed, notwithstanding his good nature, he was so troubled by the letters of the alphabet, that he grew to hate the very shape of them, an unkind feeling which, he confessed with shame, he still, to some extent, entertained. The letter M, for example, he frequently failed to recognise, because it was to him so much like W. It was only by shutting one eye and looking at both of them sideways that he at length learned to appreciate the difference. But Michael could read, and, as a matter of fact, had read portions of the Bible and the whole of the *Pilgrim's Progress*, and he could write. Speaking to me of those days, Michael observed that if there was one thing more than another he regretted, it was that he should have been removed from school before he had the chance of doing a really good multiplication sum. Daddy had hoped that Michael would have been a dispenser, but the confidential report of the teacher was so discouraging that Daddy put the lad into a canoe and took him to sea. Michael, however, soon became an expert fisherman. Three weeks after he began the business he made his father a present of a slate-coloured beaver. When he was not fishing or overhauling his tackle, Michael would weed the garden, manure the fruit trees, and do odd jobs about the house. On Sundays he was the assistant beadle. Indeed, he had no disposition and no time to be idle. Sooner than gaze into space, Michael would patch his trousers. Wherefore the town, ever hard to please, was proud of him.

Negro Nobodies

And he could thoroughly enter into the festive spirit of certain occasions, and tell a joke that was worth repeating. There are, I have heard, different opinions as to the nature and number of the qualities that constitute an excellent character. Michael, therefore, may not have been such an estimable young man. I am, however, correct in saying that he was at least honest, manly and affectionate; that he endeavoured to please his father in every respect, and to earn the good opinion of his friends.

Mary's nose was the shape of Daddy's. Otherwise she was the counterpart of her mother. She was one year younger than Michael, although, seeing them together, you would not have thought so. Mary, generally serious, looked fully four years older. If Michael, merely drinking his sugar and water in the mornings, had found it necessary to entreat Providence to remove his aunt Matilda, Mary, whose life was more or less confined to the house, had had special cause to regret the untimely death of her mother. But for this sad circumstance, her aunt Matilda would have remained at her hut fattening and tormenting other people until she died. Daddy, however, was obliged to avail himself of Matilda's assistance, as he felt he could not himself properly care the children, and as it was against his principle to invite a strange woman to sleep in his apartments. Mary first objected, with good reason, to the way in which her aunt Matilda applied a 'fine teeth' comb daily to her hair. No notice was taken of the knots. In the course of a few months, therefore, Mary became, to some extent, bald headed. Then, although she had entered her teens, her aunt insisted on making her dresses, with the result that the arm holes were invariably too large. One dress, Mary had the misfortune to hear someone say, was all arm hole. Even her father knew that her aunt Matilda was not to be trusted with the needle, because she sewed a button to his collar band which suddenly left it half an hour afterwards, in church, just as the bell stopped. Besides, her aunt Matilda was extravagant. To fry a dozen sprats, for example, she used a pint of cocoanut oil. To sweeten her mug of coffee she used, twice a day, a tablespoonful of sugar. Coffee, she declared, could never be too sweet. After insisting for a long time that she, could, she at last admitted that she could not boil an egg. When, asserting that it was hard, she broke it boldly, it turned out to be quite soft, and, perhaps, the yoke fell upon the table. When, on the other hand, believing it to be soft, she cracked it carefully, it sometimes could scarcely leave the shell. Washing, she would leave the soap in the water until it wasted. Also she ground her teeth at nights, and, during the day, ate like an elephant. Altogether her aunt Matilda caused her much unhappiness, but Mary, as far as she was able, held her peace.

Negro Nobodies

Concerning Mary's appearance there could be but one opinion; it was refined. Tall and delicate like her mother, she had a figure lacking neither dignity nor grace; and whenever I saw her, she was dressed like a lady. Mary's large black eyes were the prettiest I have ever seen. Generally speaking, a brother is wont to declare, contrary to fact, that his sister is neither good-looking nor amiable. Michael was no exception to the rule. His opinion of Mary, although not characteristically positive and extreme, I could not, with any justice to her, set down here. Mary had, nevertheless, a pretty face, and she was as sweet tempered as her mother. In company she must ever take the seat that was least conspicuous, and she was not to be seen at an unwomanly gathering, or on a questionable occasion. Ah, Mary, to think that eventually you should have experienced such an unholy thing, you, who grew in righteousness and truth, abiding by the Scriptures and knowing no evil; you, whose thoughts were whiter than the white lily, you, whose love was lovelier than the rose! But I anticipate.

In affection Mary was not found insincere by even her aunt Matilda, but she was, naturally, devoted to her father, and spent most of her time securing him those comforts which he needed. Wherefore of his two children, of whom he was justly proud, Daddy loved more the younger, Mary.

ZACCHEUS METTLE
ADDRESSES A MEETING

CHAPTER VI

I AM not likely to forget that Saturday evening, the fifteenth of June,
when, by the light of a few puny
tallow candles and a tin kerosene lamp
that smoked abominably, Zacche spoke
at length on the ways of women. For
a long while men like Daddy, Tilbert
and Binn, who were fathers, and Uttock,
Phillips and Burnet, who hoped to be
in that important position before they
died, had been having their ears troubled

103

by certain most disrespectful statements
affecting 'de soft sex them' and wedlock
generally, for which statements, as every-
body knew, Zacche Mettle, the tailor,
was responsible. So, one morning,
these men came to the conclusion that
the time had arrived when Zacche
should, publicly, either apologise for
all he had said, or emphasise his views
to his everlasting disgrace. A meeting
was therefore arranged, at which, however, Zacche was very kindly asked to
treat the subjects or subject as he
considered best. According to Zacche's
idea, the arrangement was excellent.
He, too, had for a long while not only
been hearing but seeing things which
greatly distressed him, and he had been
patiently waiting the hour and the

company when and before whom he
could deliver his views to the best
advantage. He could easily have arranged his own meeting, but how. many
would have attended? Now, however,
the platform had been placed for him;
the long-desired opportunity had been
given to him, and speak he would
'sutt'nly, like a man.' So anxious,
indeed, was he to facilitate the arrangements for the meeting that he offered
to provide the lights, which, however,
as I have hinted, were lights that
failed. His work - table he said would
hold twelve persons sitting back to
back. But this offer was declined with
thanks.

It rained heavily nearly the whole of
the day, and at eight o'clock precisely—

when, I was informed, the meeting would be opened — there was water everywhere and the heavens showed no star. But as I knew that this was no uncommon weather, I picked my path as speedily as I could to the tailor shop where, sure enough, several had already gathered. Zacche arrived late, fully intending to apologise, but, learning that they only required light, he changed his mind. The shop, for some reason or other, still leaked appreciably, and the difficulty was so to seat the people that they did not get wet. After Hooper had heard all the suggestions, he observed simply that there was such a thing as odd numbers sitting under a table. The few, therefore, who were subject to cold, or who suffered from rheumatism, sat under the table.

Negro Nobodies

Phillips, being the tallest, steadied the kerosene lamp on the top of his head. The candles, stuck in the necks of empty rum bottles, stood in line upon the table. In the semi-darkness many expressions could not be defined. Indeed, the coal-black faces in the corners of the shop could scarcely be seen, but the teeth of those who grinned seemed very white. The shadows on the walls were curious. There was little ceremony. At the commencement of these proceedings, it was the custom for the chairman to inquire whether or no the company were comfortably seated. On this occasion, therefore, Daddy called out, 'Hellick Binn, is you all right?' to which Binn, whose seat satisfied him, replied, 'First - class, Missa Daddy.' 'John Scott, my son, you have the mark?' 'Thank you kindly, Missa Daddy,' and so on; after which Zacche was asked to address the meeting. Zacche had availed himself of an exalted position, standing on a box on the table, with the candles for footlights, and he was not unembarrassed. Indeed, Burnet declared that, in the clearing of Zacche's throat, the first five words were lost, but that was not so, for Zacche spoke plainly, and here is what he said :

'Well, gentlemen, sutt'nly I am no great speaker.' (Cries of 'Don't mind that side man ;' 'Whichen we all know you is,' and, from under the table, 'Don't keep we too long all you do, my son.') 'Sutt'nly, as I say, I am no great or wonderful orator, but I am to give my views here this night, whichen is de identical truth

Negro Nobodies

from my experience, and what I have really heard in a great matter. And, sutt'nly, I have much pleasure, gentlemen, in speaking here this night upon de said great subject. (Mind you' head and that lamp, Needlecase.) Well, gentlemen, sutt'nly de subject is de ways of such persons as women, and de first thing, de correctest thing is, I think, for me just to give you a short description, from my own mind, of what such a person as a woman is. A woman, gentlemen, is· a female.' ('Whichen is de truth,' cried the company, and there· was much applause). 'And a female is sutt'nly a creature with a temper, a long tongue and a terrible weakness to wear every sailor hat and print frock her eye take a fancy upon.' (Sensation). 'Sutt'nly, there are all kinds of woman.

The Overseas Library

There is short woman and tall woman;
thin woman and stout woman; woman
with teeth (mostly jaw teeth) and woman
without any teeth at all. But I am
speaking of de generality of women
them; de woman that we meet every
day—whichen is de ordinary woman.'

'Like Rachel Uttock?' said someone
mischievously.

'Cho,' said Binn, pettishly, 'all of you
keep you'self quiet now; don't turn us
from de course of de man argument.'

'Zacche, my son,' observed Daddy, who
looked sleepy, 'I don't deny you really
make a good start, although I does not
see my way yet to agree with you.
Howsomever, proceed.'

'This creature, woman,' Zacche proceeded, 'is like a lucky bag whichen

small children buy for a quattie' (1½d.) 'because it has a pretty face upon it, and, because it is supposed to contain first-class sugar plums and, maybe, such a thing as a diamond ring. But what do de said children find? Sutt'nly, I say, what do they find? De sugar plum all make out of plaster of Paris, and de ring—well, sutt'nly, that is a kind of a hoop for de finger having de likeness of a ring and made out of a cheap brass wire. Gentlemen, it is no diamond ring at all.' (Cries of 'For true, for true, 'pon my word.') 'But, gentlemen, what can you expect for a so-so quattie? Howsomever, that is another matter. In de beginning a woman was made from de ribs of a man, Adam by name, whichen we read of in de second chapter of

Genesis de twenty second verse (correct
me, Missa Daddy, if I am wrong), and
de said woman she was made perfect
and knew no evil whatsoever. But she
listened to all de word de serpent say,
whichen we notice in de third chapter
of Genesis de sixth verse, therefore she
becomes to know evil, to teach evil, to
do evil, to even have de great likeness
of evil; and she have all those particular
faculties down to this very day. A
woman is de most perfect living instance of
pure contraryness. Altogether, gentlemen,
a woman is a petticoat full of powerful de-
struction.' (Sensation and sighs). 'Sutt'nly,
gentlemen, I hope I don't fatigue you?'

No one was feeling fatigued, so Zacche
continued,—

'Well, sutt'nly, we come now to de ways

of women. A woman, gentlemen, has
more ways than wants—whichen that is
saying an awful thing, for, sutt'nly, a
woman lives to want. In fact, there is
no counting a woman's ways. De more I
live, de more you live, de more we all
live, we are convinced that there is no
end or specification to a woman's ways.
Now, there are many old ways, but there
are a heap of new ways. Sutt'nly, de old
ways are bad ways, but, O Lord, de new
ways is de worst ways. Mind you, Hellick
Binn, hear me good what I am saying—'

'But you is an idle man, though,' replied
Binn. 'Who says I'm not hearing you?'

'Nothing, nothing, my friend,' said
Zacche quickly, 'no damage, no damage·
I only refer to you because you' face
was before me when I pronounced de

said words. Howsomever, as I was saying, there is no end to a woman's ways. But, may be, you would really like to know what is a woman's ways. Well, sutt'nly, I will tell you. But before I begin I will thank you kindly, Scotty, to pass me that can of lime water in de corner there. To talk 'pon such a thing as woman is enough to give an iron man a dry throat. . . . Thank you, brother, thank you. . . . Well, now, sutt'nly, we come to de ways of woman. A woman, gentlemen, will make an affidavit that she loves you to de bottom of her soul, and really she has no more feeling for you than a croaking lizard has for a turkey cock. That is one way, and, sutt'nly, that is a very common way. A woman will say she don't love you in de least when, all de time, she is really worshipping you down to even such a thing as you' smallest toe nail. Sutt'nly, that is an extraordinary way, but it is a way all de same. When a woman is introduced to a man she can only see his pockets them, making a note, first of all, of de size, and then whether those pockets look as if they are accustomed to carry money. Now, whether she will recognise him when she see him de second time—especially to remember his name—depends entirely upon that. Well, sutt'nly, that's another way. Supposing de man pockets look as if they can carry something better than copper, well, then de woman becomes most awfully sweet and give him such a fascinating conversation, that de poor fellow generally forget her eye is still 'pon him pocket, and he doesn't see, sutt'nly, that very often her hand come quite close to de said pocket them.'

'Then,' said Tilbert indignantly, 'does you mean to insinuate, does you mean to say that she is most like a thief?'

There was now something of a commotion, caused chiefly by three men who, as the shop had stopped leaking, must creep from under the table to stretch their legs. When order was restored, and Zacche had again sipped the lemon water, he replied that he meant 'something of de kind,' but that the said expression was what might be called 'an illustration example, meaning, sutt'nly, a figure of speech.'

Negro Nobodies

'Although,' pursued Zacche, 'women have been real thieves — whichen I can prove. I say, gentlemen, that de woman will keep on fascinating that poor man till he has to confess that he love her; then, sutt'nly, from that said day land crab in hot water is nothing to him. First is de pair of boots (generally five shillings of you' hard, hard savings), then de glove, then de bangles, then de rings, then — well, sutt'nly, hell. And that's de long and de short of it. What is marriage? Marriage is de—'

'Utter ruination of de man for ever and ever, amen!' exclaimed Uttock, who could not contain himself.

'Sutt'nly,' said Zacche, 'that is well spoken. Well, Sam did not take my advice, whichen you all know I gave him, and, gentlemen, you hear what he has to say. Sutt'nly, he can tell you de X Y Z plus de A B C of de ways of one woman, if no other. Howsomever, I shall proceed.'

But he could not, for, just then, Scott called out that there were 'two tall, female persons' at the door, who asked to be kindly admitted.

'Give de gals them room,' said Tilbert, without a second's hesitation. 'For why not? De women come to defend themselves, and they should certainly be privileged to say a few words.'

'No such thing,' shouted Zacche. 'Sutt'nly not; although de devil, or his cousin them, is always suppose to be present at a meeting.'

'Ah, Zacche, my son, my son,' said

Daddy, 'don't talk so lightly of such an awful person.'

'Whichen is woman,' replied Zacche; 'whichen is one of those women, sutt'nly, now outside de door. Well, gentle-men—' (Cries of 'Order, Order'), 'Well, gentlemen, de ways of a woman we have seen are not straight ways, but crooked ways and wicked ways. Hi, a female, whichen is a woman (don't forget that), a female, my dear friends, will have every comfort, every joy, and is yet dressing up herself at de expense of de poor man. One female I know have a way to wear her husband's full suit of clothes, as well as her own frock, to de market 'pon rainy mornings, while de poor fellow have to remain in his room, feeling a most miserable coldness without his clothes. Another female has a way, whenever she mends her husband's trousers, to leave de needle in it, whichen, de poor man confess to me, cause him a lot of uneasiness of de mind as well as de body. But, sutt'nly, these are simple ways. De chief and most destructive way is how a woman can inveigle a man to marry her; how a woman can make every sort of elevation to get a man to give her all he has, and then, suddenly, how she can turn round and give him roast horse plantain, cayenne pepper and mustard plaster all roll into one, without a rest. All you old men here present this night want to know de ways of women? Then consider what you have experienced; consider all de trouble and de expense and de devilnation generally

Negro Nobodies

from first to last, every day, every week, every month, every year, till you is now well and tired of life and craving de grave! Sutt'nly, I excuse Missa Daddy, because Miss Lucy was really an angel, God bless her two pickney them. Howsomever, a good woman, like a good fit, is de fortune of de few. And I say you young men be careful; learn, or make an effort to learn, de ways of women before you consent to say boo to one of them. Sutt'nly, single life is lonesome, but marriage bite worse than jackass.'

'Zacche, my son—'

'Sutt'nly,' pursued Zacche, in the face of Daddy's interruption, 'woman is useful, but so is dildo, whichen, as you know, makes a really first-class fence, but has more prickle and "macca," and is more ruinous to de flesh of a human person than plenty people can have a conception of. Woman, I say, is useful, but so is dildo; woman is amusing, but so is monkey, whichen is more deceitful than any other animal in this world; woman walk softly, but so do snake and scorpion; woman mean well, and so do black spiders; woman is attentive, but so is sand fly and mosquitto; woman is bewitching, but so, by all. accounts, is de very devil himself.' (General uneasiness.) 'Therefore, my dear friends, de whole thing resolve itself into this—*have nothing whatsoever to do with such a person as a woman.* You, Alexander Binn, Augustus Tilbert, Samuel Uttock and others, whichen I shall not name, that married and hang up already--- well, sutt'nly, there is nothing to be done

Negro Nobodies

for you in this world, although you can pray hard that you might not long continue subjects of such a misfortune, whichen is simply to pray that either party, either you or she, may soon cease to have an existence. But you courting gentlemen, who are not yet married and tied up, remember Samuel Uttock, I say. He is here present this night with a sorrowful face merely as an example. In conclusion I will tell you there are two particular things for a sensible man to avoid in this life, namely, poison of any sort and marriage. But sutt'nly poison is better than marriage, because in de one case you don't have time to see you' mistake before you know nothing and all is peace, while in de other case you not only see you' mistake, but you live with it, and you' two eye them is constantly upon it, and that, my son, is equal to all de fire and brimstone and hot lead and de extra special boilingnation and more down below, whichen we all have been cautioned about from de first day when we were born.' (Great excitement and loud talking, at the commencement of which two candles promptly went out, the tin kerosene lamp tried to damage the head of Needlecase, and Tilbert and another, in evident disgust, left the shop.) Then I heard the voice of Daddy, clear and resonant,—

'Children, calm you'self; calm you'self, children. There is always two sides to a question. You have heard Zacche's; well, you have yet to hear mine, whichen I will certainly give you, please God, at a suitable time by-and-by. In de mean-

time, hear well what I say — there is
woman and woman. Not every woman is
alike; Zacche himself says so. But may
be, may be, I say, you will think kindly
of *all* women, because—well, because that
person that loved you and cared you from
de days when you was little, that person
(think of it!), whom you did love better
than anybody in this world, she—your
own dear kind mother—ah, remember, *she*
was a woman.'

But Zacche had something further to say.

'Sutt'nly,' he observed, immediately
Daddy had finished speaking, 'sutt'nly I
think we have had enough of woman.
Now, gentlemen, I want to show you all
a coat whichen—'

Here nearly everyone stood up. Needle
case sat down. He wanted to know, he

said, what showing a coat had to do with the ways of woman. Daddy bid good-night. Indeed, there was a general expression of dissatisfaction, and Zacche was obliged to postpone the exhibition of his coat.

'That is nothing like de ways of woman,' said a voice, astonishingly feminine.

'No,' replied Hooper huskily, 'that is quite true, but it is everything like de ways of man, especially a little man with sense, like Zacche. Hi, of course, I thought you all knew that. And now, gentlemen, I wish you all a pleasant night's rest. I, at least, am going home (I don't know what you all going to do), for de oil in de lamp is done.'

So the meeting broke up, each man moving straightway to his abode.

A 'YOUNG LADY'

CHAPTER VII

A 'YOUNG LADY'

PORT ANTONIO, in those days, had
few 'young ladies,' or Zacche must
soon have been teased to perdition. But
of these young ladies—so called because
they were of a fast set — Irene, or, as
she was commonly called, 'Hireen' Macgregor, was . perhaps the most notorious.
Irene was interesting and no mistake.
Although her hair was cut close because,
even soaked in castor oil, it was difficult
to comb, and although she had long arms
and a mouth which I am glad I am not

I   129

scarcely a thing from morning. For example, de brush is back of de door, de dirt is on de floor and—'

Irene needed no second hint. She took the brush and the bit of old corn bag that served as a duster, and, in less than ten minutes, she made the place as clean and tidy as it could be.

'Well,' said Irene.

But Zacche answered not.

Then Irene, thinking to spite him, stepped out of the shop and bid him good-morning.

'I am leaving, do you hear?.'

'Mind you'self,' was the unexpected reply, which meant: many thanks for all you have done, very many thanks for all you intended to do, hope you will get home safely, hope to heaven I shall never see your face again — which meant a good deal, of course.

'And de bangle?' she asked.

'Sutt'nly, I sold it yesterday,' he said, and went on sewing.

Irene was of use to him, and, what would not then have been believed, he was a great admirer of 'de soft sex them.'

It will be remembered that in the heat of the meeting, when Zacche was making some most eloquent observations, Scott stopped him to announce that two tall female persons at the door kindly asked admission. Irene was one of them. She had thoroughly discussed the subject on which Zacche was to speak, and had re-solved, on gaining admission, to say a few words on behalf of her much-abused sex. Foiled in this excellent purpose, however, she determined to see Zacche, the rascal, as soon as possible, and to give him beans. Also she wanted to borrow a bangle, of some value, and pretty, which

Zacche possessed. On the following morning, therefore, she walked boldly into the tailor shop, to the astonishment of Zacche, who believed that she was on a visit to a cousin who was married and lived in Manchioneal. So astonished indeed was Zacche that he closed the scissors at the wrong place on a sleeve and completely spoilt it.

'See here,' said Irene, 'why you wouldn't let me in last night, eh? . . . Just look at him, de picture of a rat bat.'

Zacche held up the sleeve.

'Well, sutt'nly,' said he, 'I think I would say good - morning — whichen is manners.'

'Well, see here,' said Irene, 'good-morning, good - morning, good - morning, good-morning, Mista Zacche; I hope you

CHAPTER VIII

SARAH HUTCHINSON, an attentive girl in the Sunday school, was confirmed before she was fourteen years old, and from that day Christ Church, Port Antonio, knew no more enthusiastic member. Like Michael and a score of others, Sarah had had trouble with the alphabet, and would have retreated from the field had not her ambition urged her to victory. That was a sweet story about the Lord Jesus Christ, and she would read it for herself. Her chief ambition, how-

151

supposed to ask you anything about garments them that I like — with you' forwardness.'

'Make I measure you then,' said Zacche.

Irene had not anticipated this move, and it considerably affected her plans. In her embarrassment she sat down, but immediately rose and backed out of the shop, for Zacche, tape-line in hand, was evidently bent on business.

'Stop it, I say,' she cried, 'see here, stop it, I say. Stop it now; no nonsense. I am not making a piece of fun. Please to leave me alone, and let me go on with what I am asking you. You ought to be ashamed of you'self. Hi, you well and forward. Am I playing with you?'

Negro Nobodies

'Well, sutt'nly, come now,' said the little tailor, plainly put out, 'come now, stop you' talking. I have no business with you here. Walk out of my shop, I say! Sutt'nly whichen is more indecent, you to come here to ask me to make you a trousers, or me to request you to make me measure you?'

'Done, done, see here, done,' pleaded Irene, 'done, my sweetie marsa; my sugar candy, I beg you' pardon. Don't mind about de trousers. Make us forget all about it. See here, I was only making fun—'pon my word, Hi, now, could I wear trousers? After I am not a male.'

'Well, sutt'nly, you is now talking like a sensible person,' said Zacche, 'although you is nothing but a female—don't forget that little mongrel were settling a difference on the subject of a bone, and there was another dog looking on compassionately. 'Mass Jim' was carefully weighing ground coffee to be put in little paper bags for retail, while a boy on his left served cheap cheese to those who called for it. Seated on an old mahogany chair, beside a stall on which were a bucket of water and dozens of bottled cool drink, Mother Bet was polishing her teeth with a chewstick, when there was a loud cry, followed by the words, shrilly uttered,—

'I say that now, now, *now* de time has come when you must turn from your sins. Judgment is coming, my dear, sweet, sisters and brothers. O repent ye, repent ye, for de Kingdom of Heaven is at hand!'

Negro Nobodies

Surrounded by heaps of yam, plantain, cocoa, breadfruit, kallaloo, akee, limes, naseberries and other fruit, her head tied with a large white handkerchief, Sarah Hutchinson, the prophet, stood waving her hands to a number of people, chiefly women, who were gazing at her.

'O yes, O yes,' she pursued, 'the Kingdom of Heaven is at hand, prepare ye, prepare ye the way for de coming of de Lord! O all ye people that have lived in iniquity and sin, O all ye people cover you' face, turn you' head from de everlasting fire that is before you! The trumpet shall sound, the bugles shall blow, the heavens shall open, and you shall see de Lord in glory, and you shall be called upon for judgment. Wherefore I say unto you, repent ye, repent ye, before it is

'Well, sutt'nly, so you are, my friend, so you are; and a woman is a female, and a female is a person, and a *person* is—well,' said Zacche, 'a *person*, sutt'nly, is de devil—whichen we all know.'

'And I am a beautiful woman,' added Irene.

'And who,' cried Zacche, 'who says so besiden you'self, my friend? Who says so? Who—'

He paused, for, in his excitement, he dropped his needle and must look for it.

'Well, now,' said he, 'sutt'nly, you see, talking to you I have lost my needle.'

'No, indeed you haven't,' said Irene, 'here it is.' And, picking it up, she handed it to him.

Negro Nobodies

'When a person—' began Zacche.

'Well, certainly, I think I would say "thank you," which is manners,' said Irene.

Zacche was instantly on his feet and bowed low.

'I ask you' pardon,' said he. 'Sutt'nly, Miss Hireen Macgregor, I thank you.'

But in this effort to be courteous his work fell to the ground, and on taking it up again he was not a little distressed to find that a portion of the serge was soiled. Irene was not inclined to be sympathetic. She had visited Zacche principally to give him beans, had utterly failed to do so, and was, therefore, glad of any circumstance that annoyed him. But Irene was bent upon having the bangle, and so she must adopt an attitude handkerchief more securely round her head, but when she heard her name called she rose quickly, her hands trembling and her eyes having the expression of one insane.

'What are ye all gathering here for?' she shouted. 'As lambs that come to de slaughter? Go your ways, I say, go your ways, my children. There is a time coming when no man can work. The Lord He says I am not of this world, I and my Father are one. Eh? You can dispute that? Is that not gospel? Is that not, I say, de blessëd truth——'

'Cho, done, done,' once more interposed Mother Bet, 'done, Sarah. A ripe woman like you should know better. You tell us all that already, and, moreover, this is not de said time for prayer-meeting.' Then, turning to the crowd, she remarked:

'Some one of you must have been troubling her.'

'See here, Mother Bet,' said Esther Morgan, Binn's cousin, 'see here, you hear me, mam, they *do* trouble her. Rebecca Spratt, who you see just gone to de beef stall over there, she and Hireen and another gal been ask Miss Sarah all sort of questions, till de poor woman don't know what to say.'

'Oh, what de devil are *you* saying?' said Irene sharply. 'I and you is company? You well and forward. What you know? It concern you?'

'Concern me, yes,' snapped Esther. 'No (was it not) you been ask Miss Sarah questions them so make her answer you until she bawl out all of a sudden?'

'Well, certainly, it is none of *your*

'Sutt'nly, de said thing I say,' replied Zacche.

'What did you say?' she asked. 'Indeed, you don't know what you said. I suppose you will tell me you sleep well at night now?'

'Well, sutt'nly, I do not,' he answered, with a mischievous twinkle, 'whichen *you* should know.'

'Oh, go to the devil with you' forwardness,' cried Irene. 'What I know about you? I have anything to do with you?'

Zacche yawned. It was time, he thought, that he went on with his work. So he said:

'I thank you kindly to move out of de light. Sutt'nly you is good - looking, all de same I can't see through you.'

Irene was tickled. Nevertheless, surveying him, she sneered :

'Humph, and you is really beautiful, and lovely, and sweet, all to you' nose.' Then, smiling, she added, 'But see here, never mind, you want me to mix some lime juice for you?'

Zacche looked at her.

'Sutt'nly, I have no objection,' he said.

Irene now seemed in excellent humour, and soon made the drink. Handing it to him she was a little disappointed to see that he did not immediately swallow it. Having, however, done him a kindness, she had no hesitation in saying :

'See here, I am taking de bangle again, do you hear? You will lend it to me?'

'Well, sutt'nly,' said he, 'you don't do

K   145 scarcely a thing from morning. For example, de brush is back of de door, de dirt is on de floor and—'

Irene needed no second hint. She took the brush and the bit of old corn bag that served as a duster, and, in less than ten minutes, she made the place as clean and tidy as it could be.

'Well,' said Irene.

But Zacche answered not.

Then Irene, thinking to spite him, stepped out of the shop and bid him good-morning.

'I am leaving, do you hear?'

'Mind you'self,' was the unexpected reply, which meant: many thanks for all you have done, very many thanks for all you intended to do, hope you will get home safely, hope to heaven I shall never see your face again — which meant a good deal, of course.

'And de bangle?' she asked.

'Sutt'nly, I sold it yesterday,' he said, and went on sewing.

THE PROPHET, SARAH

CHAPTER VIII

SARAH HUTCHINSON, an attentive girl in the Sunday school, was confirmed before she was fourteen years old, and from that day Christ Church, Port Antonio, knew no more enthusiastic member. Like Michael and a score of others, Sarah had had trouble with the alphabet, and would have retreated from the field had not her ambition urged her to victory. That was a sweet story about the Lord Jesus Christ, and she would read it for herself. Her chief ambition, how-

151

ever, was to save souls for the Master's kingdom. Had Daddy been the beadle in those days he would have warned Sarah against 'de pride and temper and general contraryness and misery that comes of a too free reading of such a powerful book as de Bible,' but Pine, who was old and saw little, said nothing. So Sarah spelt and stumbled from Genesis to Revelations and from Revelations to Genesis, backwards and forwards, until there came a day when she decided to have a prayer - meeting on her own account. Mother Bet has assured me that the idea gave pleasure to them all. Mr Denbore, the rector at that time, was greatly in favour of it. He thought it a fine example set by a sincere Christian, to whom the Lord had given spirit with

the understanding also, and he said
Sarah's modesty withal pleased him much.
But at last the woman was carried away
by the sublimity of her work, by the
magnificence of the message she was
charged to deliver, and suddenly, one
Saturday morning, she commenced to
prophesy. It occurred in the market,
where Sarah kept a stall, and where,
when she was not making or 'crying' sugar
candy, she sold ground provisions and
fruit.

The market was full. Binn, who had
beached a fine canoe-load of fish, stood in
his usual place by the south gate, and was
endeavouring to convince the rector's cook
that, for sixpence, two small live snappers
were better than five large dead ones.
Elliot, the butcher, switch in hand, and a

little mongrel were settling a difference on the subject of a bone, and there was another dog looking on compassionately. ' Mass Jim' was carefully weighing ground coffee to be put in little paper bags for retail, while a boy on his left served cheap cheese to those who called for it. Seated on an old mahogany chair, beside a stall on which were a bucket of water and dozens of bottled cool drink, Mother Bet was polishing her teeth with a chewstick, when there was a loud cry, followed by the words, shrilly uttered,—

' I say that now, now, *now* de time has come when you must turn from your sins. Judgment is coming, my dear, sweet, sisters and brothers. O repent ye, repent ye, for de Kingdom of Heaven is at hand !'

Negro Nobodies

Surrounded by heaps of yam, plantain, cocoa, breadfruit, kallaloo, akee, limes, naseberries and other fruit, her head tied with a large white handkerchief, Sarah Hutchinson, the prophet, stood waving her hands to a number of people, chiefly women, who were gazing at her.

'O yes, O yes,' she pursued, 'the Kingdom of Heaven is at hand, prepare ye, prepare ye the way for de coming of de Lord! O all ye people that have lived in iniquity and sin, O all ye people cover you' face, turn you' head from de everlasting fire that is before you! The trumpet shall sound, the bugles shall blow, the heavens shall open, and you shall see de Lord in glory, and you shall be called upon for judgment. Wherefore I say unto you, repent ye, repent ye, before it is

indeed too late. He that believeth in
me—'

'Never mind, never mind,' said Mother
Bet, who, directly she heard the cry, had
pushed her way through the crowd to
Sarah's elbow, 'never mind, never mind,
my daughter. Never mind—sh—sh—sh—
that will do. Done, done; we is all well
acquainted with our iniquity and sin, and
we are really praying to de Lord for for-
giveness. Done, done, you hear? Don't
say anything more.'

Then addressing the crowd she said :

'But who disturb her? Who raise her?
Rachel Uttock, and you, Miss Hireen, you
couldn't go you' ways and leave de poor
creature alone?'

At that moment Irene was more concerned with the movements of the doctor's

coachman, whom she saw in the distance, than with either Sarah or Mother Bet; consequently she took no notice of what the latter said. Rachel, however, replied not a little angrily :

'See here, I beg you please to leave me alone this blessèd morning. You see me interfering with her? You see me have any conversation with anybody? After I just—just this minute come here. I thank you kindly to leave me alone.'

'See here,' said another woman, 'don't have no contention, See here, Mother Bet, for true and true, Rachel Uttock have nothing to do with it. Ask Miss Sarah, and let her tell you.'

Sarah, on the interruption of Mother Bet, had resumed her seat, tying the white handkerchief more securely round her head, but when she heard her name called she rose quickly, her hands trembling and her eyes having the expression of one insane.

'What are ye all gathering here for?' she shouted. 'As lambs that come to de slaughter? Go your ways, I say, go your ways, my children. There is a time coming when no man can work. The Lord He says I am not of this world, I and my Father are one. Eh? You can dispute that? Is that not gospel? Is that not, I say, de blessëd truth—'

'Cho, done, done,' once more interposed Mother Bet, 'done, Sarah. A ripe woman like you should know better. You tell us all that already, and, moreover, this is not de said time for prayer-meeting.' Then, turning to the crowd, she remarked:

158

Negro Nobodies

'Some one of you must have been troubling her.'

'See here, Mother Bet,' said Esther Morgan, Binn's cousin, 'see here, you hear me, mam, they *do* trouble her. Rebecca Spratt, who you see just gone to de beef stall over there, she and Hireen and another gal been ask Miss Sarah all sort of questions, till de poor woman don't know what to say.'

'Oh, what de devil are *you* saying?' said Irene sharply. 'I and you is company? You well and forward. What you know? It concern you?'

'Concern me, yes,' snapped Esther. 'No (was it not) you been ask Miss Sarah questions them so make her answer you until she bawl out all of a sudden?'

'Well, certainly, it is none of *your*

business,' said Irene stiffly, 'so please to walk off. Mother Bet, you make Miss Sarah talk, mam. It's talk she want to talk.'

'But, Lord,' exclaimed a little woman who had been standing for some time with three plantains in her hand, 'good Lord, am I to stand here all de day? Miss Sarah, serve me de three gill worth of plantain and make me go my ways. All of you people have nothing to do here, or you would not stand up and trouble what don't concern you.'

'What you want?' asked Sarah, almost shrieking.

'Do so—so three gills (twopence farthing) of plantain,' replied the woman. 'And, see here, after I am not a pig, what you bawl at me for? Serve me the plantain, I say, and make me go my ways.'

'I am not serving no plantain,' said Sarah, grabbing the plantains which the woman held. 'I am here to warn you all of the wrath that is to come.' And she sat down and sighed.

'Poor thing,' muttered the little woman, 'she must be mad, she *must* be mad.'

'She is mad, yes,' said a boy mischievously. 'Look 'pon her eye, don't you see it favour rolling calf? They should take her up and send her home.'

'You, sir,' exclaimed Mother Bet, 'if I hear you say that word again, I give you such a flogging that you never forget it.'

'But who is he?' inquired Esther Morgan.

'Is it not Miss Aitcheson last boy

pickney?' replied Miss Harris, who knew everything, 'and de most hurtful thing is, that his father was such a quiet man; don't trouble anybody, and he and Miss Sarah been know one another well, being they confirm de same day.' Then, lowering her voice, she said to Mother Bet, 'But you know, Bet, for true and true, Sarah eye *do* look funny. I notice it this three days now, and to-day she is well and excited.'

'But she is not mad, mam,' answered Mother Bet, 'only they keep on teasing her. . . . Sarah,' addressing the prophet, 'don't you see de creature is waiting for her plantain?'

'For it shall be a time of woe,' observed Sarah, with dignity, 'a time and a season of fasting and repentance.'

Negro Nobodies

'But—' began Mother Bet.

'Not a time of joy,' pursued Sarah, 'but a time of fasting and repentance. In de 41st chapter of de book of de prophet Isaiah—'

'But done,' pleaded Mother Bet, 'done; do my love, done. Don't you hear?'

'She is mad, yes,' bawled the boy, and he dodged under the stall.

'Mad? No. She no mad.' This was a short, slim, Coolie man whom they called 'Johnson-come-Calcutta.' 'What for she mad? Mad? No. . . . Hi, salaam, Miss Sarah, salaam. Johnson-come-Cal-cutta side—hi—him buy good kellaloo—hi! Give me sixpence wut good kellaloo—quick! Sun hot this morning, my bakkara' ('backra' or white man).

The Overseas Library

Sarah looked steadily at the Coolie for a second or two, and then, smiling, handed him the sixpence worth of good kallaloo.

'And quattie' (three halfpence) 'worth of akee for me,' said someone hoarsely.

'And see here, mam, you make farthing worth of yam?' asked another.

'Hi, but serve us, can't you!' exclaimed a third.

Sarah, however, staring at the roof of the market, seemed to hear no one.

'Well,' observed the akee customer, walking away, 'if she don't mad, she favour mad, and she can keep her damn akee them.'

Meanwhile the crowd had increased, and the opinion was being freely expressed that Sarah Hutchinson had gone mad. Daddy, who had come into the market by the merest chance, and Hooper, who had seen the crowd as he passed Binn's stall, approached just as the Coolie was leaving. Daddy immediately proceeded to gather information, but Hooper must first salute Johnson.

'Hi, Johnson,' said he, 'hi, man, you is going very fast with all that kellaloo. Let me see what you have there. Hi, yes!'

The Coolie grinned, but would not stop. Hooper then addressed Irene.

'Well, now,' said he, 'what's all this, what's all this? Hi, Irene gal, you is looking as fresh as a lignum vitæ blossom with a bee upon it. Hi, yes! What you is doing here?'

'See here,' she replied, 'don't ask me

165

anything, for I am not going to answer you. See Mother Bet there, ask her.'

Hooper, however, had no occasion to ask, for Sarah again raised her voice.

'Ye have betrayed me,' she cried. 'Ye have crucified me, but my blood is shed for you all, all, *all.* So spoke de Lord. "Come unto me all ye that labour and are heavy laden, and I will give you rest." My brethren, I have exhorted you before to walk in righteousness. I have called upon you to turn ye from you' evil ways, but have you done so? Now is de great time coming. You will be judged, I say; you will be weighed in de great balance and found wanting.'

'Hi,' said Hooper. 'Gead, she is giving us a whole sermon and a benediction as well—hi, yes! Then she is going to tell us all about milk and honey, and now *that's* what I like.'

But Daddy was much distressed. Tears were in his eyes as he laid his hand on Sarah's shoulder.

'My daughter,' said he tenderly, 'let us pray together, but not now. Calm you'self; de Lord is supporting you. Have patience; indeed, all will be well.'

Sarah listened to him with interest, and, when he had finished, said :

'All will be well, say you? But de Philistine them is against us. Howsomever, de race is not to de swift nor de battle to de strong!'

Daddy thought he would exercise even greater tact.

'Miss Hutcheson,' said he, pointing to a heap of provisions, 'those are fine yams you have there.'

Sarah smiled.

'This long time you never come to de market, Missa Daddy, till to-day you come. Well, I am really pleased to see you. You know I have a dream last night? Yes, Missa Daddy, it has come to pass, and I saw a great, shining light, and Moses and Abraham and Isaac and Elijah and Paul — oh, yes, oh, yes —and Peter and de whole of them, Jew and Gentile. And I get a message for de whole of us. What you say to that?'

Daddy did not reply, and Sarah proceeded to reheap some provisions which had been scattered. The crowd had now satisfied its curiosity, and begun to disperse. A few pressed closer to Sarah to make purchases, and they were not long kept waiting. Several, however— including Daddy, Miss Harris, Esther Morgan, Irene Macgregor and Hooper— removed to Mother Bet's stall, where, as Hooper suggested, they could all give sermons upon Sarah at the same time. Miss Harris spoke first, and it was while Mother Bet uncorked a bottle of 'cool drink' for Daddy.

'You know, Bet,' said Miss Harris, 'I really think a woman don't have a natural constitution and a mind for preaching, and woman them shouldn't study de Bible too close, whichen, as is well known, it is a very powerful and mysterious book. Then, you know, Sarah mother,

they say, been dead in a mad-house;
and all this reading and preaching and
de said inheritance from her mother going
to turn her head for ever and ever, amen.'

'Miss Bet,' said Daddy, 'your cool
drink does you credit, whichen all of us
is prepared to pay you de same compliment. Miss Harris, I agree with you;
woman don't really make for preaching.
You will remember Missa Blackburn
sermon de other day. And, mark you,
Sarah is not a strong woman. Then
you must remember she has grown up
in de Church, and confirm in de Church,
and she has been a member all these
years—all de way from Missa Denbore
and old Pine — and she accustomed to
prayer meeting, so her mind is constantly
upon de Gospel without a rest.'

Negro Nobodies

'Her mind was upon something else already,' remarked Hooper. 'Hi, yes, but de something went away with his regiment and died in Africa, and that is de first time Sarah has such a thing as a feeling to prophesy.'

'See here,' said Irene, 'that is what you are always thinking of.'

'Well, I don't say no,' replied Hooper. 'De only thing is, of course, we are talking about Sarah and not about me.'

'She don't mad,' protested Mother Bet, 'but she get well excited, being de morning is really warm and they keep on ask her questions.'

'She says she had a dream,' said Esther. 'Was that not what she told Missa Daddy?'

'Now, that is pure madness,' observed

Miss Harris. 'You think Sarah has eyes to see a shining light?'

'Well,' said Hooper, 'I don't know about that, for she has just seen Missa Daddy, Mother Bet, Irene and myself, and we are de shining light for de time being of Port Antonio.'

Irene smiled, and even Mother Bet seemed tickled by the compliment, but Daddy thought otherwise.

'Charlie, my son,' said he, looking Hooper full in the face, 'you' tongue is running easy, but you' heart is heavy. Be careful. Don't make sport of poor Sarah. She is really an understanding woman, really a woman of faith and truth, and de Lord will support her.'

'Hi, yes,' said Hooper, very solemnly.

'Then I hear say that for de last

three night now she can't sleep at all,' Esther informed the company; 'and I hear say she call Missa Blackburn name and clap her hands and sing hymns them.'

'Now,' exclaimed a little woman, with a ginger-coloured complexion, 'now, that's de same thing now; and that's how some people them tell lie. Mother Barnet tell me say that she hear say Sarah get up at night to receive spirit them. Then she clap her hands to tell de spirit when she is ready, then they all sing hymns.'

'But is that not pure foolishness?' said a girl. 'After spirits them can't sing.'

'Sing, of course,' declared another. 'What *you* know about them?'

Esther would gladly have expressed her

opinion upon this particular point had she not been prevented by 'Mistriss' Walters—a fat little gossip—who, just at this moment, made her way into the centre of the crowd.

'All of you here come with me,' urged Mistriss Walters, almost breathless with excitement, 'all of you here come with me. Come quick; come hear Miss Hutcheson! My good Miss Bet' (turning to that individual), 'poor Sarah can't be in her right senses. . . . Well, well, well, look how me an old somebody live 'till this day to hear yam and plaintain and preaching and praying all mix up together. All of you come quick!'

Several of the unkind and curious were ready to move immediately, but Daddy entreated them not to do so.

Negro Nobodies

'Mistriss Walters make a mistake,' said he, 'whichen she will confess, so I will ask you all very kindly to go your ways. Don't harrass de poor creature again. . . . Hireen, my daughter, show them de way. Miss Bet, Broderick here will thank you kindly for a pan of cool drink. Esther, may be Binn would like to ask you a question. Charlie, my son, I will see you later. Miss Harris, I will say a few words with you if you please, so just take a step this side.'

In this way Daddy soon cleared the crowd, and, taking the arm of Miss Harris, walked across to Sarah's stall. Mistriss Walters had not exaggerated. Even before the couple approached close enough to be seen, Sarah was heard jumbling, in a manner not a little humorous, familiar phrases of Scripture, with short sentences common to the market.

'Comfort ye, comfort ye,' she pursued, with singular earnestness, 'comfort ye, my people saith—gal, I sell nothing but dry yam, and I sell it cheap. And Paul said unto Agrippa—Well, if you don't like de yam them leave them, I am not begging you to buy any. Hi, what a thing now. . . . Cast thy bread upon de waters and it shall return unto you—I say these three pieces here for sixpence, those three there for sixpence, and these two for threepence. It is good dry yam, I tell you. . . . Whosoever will—'

The couple drew a little nearer.

'Missa Daddy,' whispered Miss Harris, 'what you think of it, eh?'

Negro Nobodies

'What I think?' replied Daddy sadly. 'Well, I think and I see till my heart is full, Miss Harris. Sarah—whichen you know she is no common woman—Sarah, alas! come this day to a very sad weakness. Howsomever, who shall question de ways of de Lord? I am saying, Miss Harris, that you would think de devil had no control over a person so long as de holy Spirit dwell within her, but we really see to de contrary. De devil, we see, disturb Sarah's mind for her to minister no more against him. De devil, always de devil, Miss Harris, wherever you turn—as it was in de beginning, is now, and ever shall be, world without end—'

'Amen,' said Miss Harris.

'Whichen is de conclusion of de whole matter,' said Daddy and he sighed.

The Overseas Library

'Nevertheless and notwithstanding,' observed Miss Harris, 'and asking you to pardon me for being so bold, Missa Daddy, if I was you I would take home Miss Hutcheson instead of standing up here behind her back so sorrowful, but doing nothing.'

'Whichen is a sensible word,' admitted Daddy, 'and so I thank you kindly, Miss Harris, to mind the provisions them while I take home de poor creature and see Missa Blackburn to make de arrangements.'

To induce Sarah to leave the stall, however, was no simple matter. Was it the will of the Lord that she should leave the stall? she asked. And now Daddy's courteous firmness would have surprised a stranger. At last Sarah seemed to see the kindness and the wisdom of his words, and, taking his hand as a child would take the hand of her father, the 'prophet' walked quietly away.

THE SHADOW OF A SIN·

CHAPTER IX

THE heat that day had baked the violet bed, and I was emptying the third pan of water upon it when old 'Mistriss' Pengelly rapped sharply at the garden gate to tell me of her son's arrival. 'My son come, busha, my son come,' she cried. 'Busha, Reggie come, sa, and he really look handsome, and I am indeed well pleased to see him.'

'Mistriss' Pengelly, a respectable widow, had four sons, but of these there was one only, a fine young man, of whom she

could justly be proud. The other three
had tempers and vices, and although their
mother loved them so dearly that she
could not see the whole number or the
seriousness of their faults, it was no secret
that these three sons caused her a good
deal of anxiety. The youngest, Reginald,
had the most uncontrollable temper, which
deprived him of work very soon after he
had obtained it, and which threatened
entirely to disfigure his life. But he had
such a kind heart, and, though black,
such fine features and such manners, that
he made many friends—chiefly among the
'young gentlemen' or common swells of
the town. He was no favourite with the
old and sober heads, however, nor with
such men as Binn, Hooper and Zacche
who thought him intolerable. When,

therefore, on finding little employment in the town, he determined to see a bit of the world, 'missis queen and all de prince and pretty princess them,' and it was likely he would not return, there was a feeling of regret among his friends, and his mother cried, but Binn and others expressed their satisfaction and the hope that, if his temper did not lead him on to murder and hanging abroad, Reginald would some day come back to them a quiet, wise and well-behaved man. All the money and the means necessary for his passage in the schooner *Esther Bell*, to Boston, his mother and Daddy found for him. Indeed, Daddy persuaded the rector to give Reginald a letter to a clergyman in the States who would surely help him in the hour of need. Soon

after the schooner sailed, a report was
mysteriously mouthed about the town that
•she had foundered, and the distress of
Mistriss Pengelly at the death of this
estimable son was painful to witness.
The arrival of another schooner, however,
with a letter from Reginald in Boston,
soon dispelled his mother's fears. For a
few months afterward, he wrote her
regularly, but these letters told a miserable
tale. He could get no work and was
starving. Could his mother lend him a
few shillings? He would be sure to return them with love and interest. And
the mother was at her wit's end to find
the money. Still, she sent him the few
shillings, 'and so that you keep a good
boy, my son,' she dictated, 'and love and
fear de Lord and walk in his ways, no

trouble to return de money, whichen I give you for you'self.' Then three mails arrived and there was no letter, and, as· the postman rapped less at her door, you might have seen the old woman, her face careworn and wet with tears, calling at the post office to inquire why Reginald had not sent her a letter.

Speaking to me of the distress of Mistriss Pengelly at this time, Daddy took the opportunity to observe, with fervour, that there was nothing in this world more permanently beneficial to the body, the mind and the soul than prayer offered daily, on bended knees, from the lowest bottom of the heart. The Lord, added Daddy, did not allow Mistriss Pengelly to suffer long, having taken due notice of her prayers, for she soon received tidings of her son, who had left Boston for Colon, there to make a fortune and a home. The news was confirmed by a letter from Reginald who, however, was in ill health and debt. Mother Bet, learning of this fresh appeal (for Reginald had, of course, appealed for help) was bold enough to remark that if Reginald had a face, he certainly had no conscience, and that his mother would be a great fool to again help him. Mother Bet protested that he was not sick at all, but playing 'grand man' in Colon, whilst his eldest brother slaved in Port Antonio to support the family, which was a burning shame. And Mother Bet was supported in this opinion by many. But Mistriss Pen-

gelly believed otherwise. Poor Reginald
was dying in a strange land among
strangers, she pleaded, and so won the
sympathies of several people. Money
must be raised to relieve him, and,
for this purpose, there was a great sale
of Mistriss Pengelly's guava jelly and
cocoanut cake. Zacche filled his stomach
for three. days and three nights with
' grater ' cake, 'sutt'nly,' said he, ' not
for de boy himself — whichen he is a
scamp, as we all know, but for de sake
of his poor old mother going fast to
her grave, and taking a last experience
of this sorrowful world.' The money
thus raised was forwarded without delay,
to be returned, Reginald wrote, with more
which he was going to make to comfort his dear mother in her declining days.

The Overseas Library

Reginald remained in Colon for a couple of years, during which time he made, but with little success, many more appeals to his family for money—during which time also he lived a life of extravagant pleasure and acquired vices of a refined kind. But the day dawned, to be sure, when he was advised to leave that country. , Borrowing, therefore, all the money he could, he set sail at night for Jamaica. Before leaving, however, he informed his mother of a certain small fortune which he had made and as good as lost, but that he was returning home to let her enjoy the few dollars that were left.

Reginald arrived in Port Antonio from Kingston one fine afternoon in May, to the astonishment of Uttock who, hurrying to the Reservoir, was the first to see him. 'Hi, so you is with we again,' was all Uttock had time to say. Reginald next met Needlecase Phillips striding straight for Titchfield with a pair of boots under his arm. Phillips stopped. 'Well now coo' (look at) 'Reginald!' he exclaimed and strode on. But he took the news with him to Titchfield, and in ten minutes Mistriss Pengelly and the friends in town were gathered together to welcome Reginald. It was an afternoon to be remembered, the pleasure marred only, as Mistriss Pengelly said, by the fact that Reginald's brothers, working them at different places in the parish, were not there to receive him. After an embrace in which she cried for joy, excitement lent Mistriss

The Overseas Library

Pengelly strength to walk briskly up
the hill to the rector's door and to my
garden gate. Then she returned to
the house where she found Reginald
admiring his features in a broken looking-
glass and commenting on the general
shabbiness of the place. Later, Daddy
called to welcome his godson.

' My son—' he began.

' No preaching, old man, I hope,' interposed Reginald.

Daddy was surprised and not a little
pained, but you would scarcely have
known it.

' My son,' said he, ' I am indeed glad
to see you. You really grow tall and
handsome and you look very well.'

Reginald beamed, and drew his stool
nearer the beadle.

Negro Nobodies

'I am really glad to see you myself, Missa Daddy,' said he. 'You have grown old, but old age, as you know, is honour; honour is de richness of de soul; and de soul is precious in de sight of the Lord.'

Mistriss Pengelly, putting supper on the table, straightened herself with pride. In all her life she had not heard words as eloquent as these. Daddy, too, thought kindly.

'I am saying, Reggie,' he remarked, 'you' connection with de Church in Colon, but more especially you' mother and our prayers, has been of some assistance to you. Now, I am well thankful for that, and I hope to see you, my son, an everlasting credit, like you' poor dead father, in this said town of Port Antoney.'

The Overseas Library

Reginald gripped the old man's hand, and Daddy was satisfied. The truth is, Daddy was too charitable and therefore too blind to see that Reginald was a humbug.

The conversation now turned on the subject of Reginald's experiences abroad, and he spoke so modestly and sensibly —giving Heaven credit, like a Christian, for whatever health and prosperity he had had—that his mother embraced him again and again, and Daddy left the house with the conviction that Reginald was one of the finest young men he had ever known. Indeed, Daddy did not wait until the following morning to give Michael and Mary his impressions —to give Mary particularly who, he was aware, had always had a kind feeling for Reginald. If Daddy had been observant he would have seen that Mary listened to him that evening with unusual attention; that, in fact, she seemed peculiarly pleased at what he said. The next day Reginald called at the cottage, and, Daddy and Michael being out, was entertained by Mary. He was dressed in his best blue suit, wore his heavy 'gold' chain and ring, and endeavoured to look like a wealthy gentleman. He is more handsome than ever, thought Mary, and such a nice fellow. When Daddy returned he found them seated at the table, with the large Bible between them, discussing the Scriptures. Now this was a sight that pleased the beadle. If it should come to pass that this new Reginald, who was so respectable, should marry Mary, how happy he would be. So Daddy lit his pipe and smoked, and the smoke was sweet. Reginald then became intimate with the family, making Mary presents and treating Daddy with much kindness and respect. With Michael, however, he was less friendly, for Reginald fancied that Michael suspected him. Meanwhile the joy of Mistriss Pengelly was unspeakable. Robert, Alexander and Frederick had come to town and given their brother a hearty welcome. Robert, who still supported his mother, was no longer the pride of the family. Reginald was the pride of the family: Reginald with the handsome face, the ring, the heavy 'gold' chain— and the score of vices. Reginald is

good, said his mother. He even pre-
sumed to attend the Communion —
evidence of his piety which Daddy
deemed indisputable. Reginald, however,
still showed that sort of contempt for
straightforwardness and that impertinent
independence which Binn, and men like
him, so disliked. And now Reginald
displayed his fine clothes and watch and
chain on every occasion — especially on
Sundays and in a manner to indicate
that he was the most important person
in the town. So Binh and Hooper and
Zacche abided their time.

The intimacy with Mary plainly ripened
into courtship, yet, strangely enough,
Daddy took no steps, as usual, to hasten
the marriage. And now Zacche, a keen
observer and logician of a kind, who saw

The Overseas Library

Reginald and Mary more frequently than they thought they were seen—Zacche had an idea. In short, he was convinced that Reginald was very carefully planning to seduce Mary, and Zacche must, as the saying is, put a spoke in the villain's wheel. Meeting Michael one evening after service, he asked Michael if he could tell him positively whether Reginald was courting Mary.

'Sutt'nly,' added Zacche, 'that's what I hear, but report, like female, is not to be relied upon. Sutt'nly I don't want you to tell me a secret, but if you' tongue is really loose—well, sutt'nly, speak out like a man.'

Michael replied that he believed they were engaged, and attempted to pass on. But Zacche held him, for he had something more to say.

Negro Nobodies

'Well, look here,' said he sternly, 'open
you' eye and you' father eye, Michael
Rutherford, although sutt'nly don't say I
say so. One thing I have to say, and it
is this: a Colon man don't live in Colon
and wear Colon watch and chain and ring
and blue suit for nothing. Well, sutt'nly
that's all. Good-night.'

Michael's suspicions were therefore
strengthened, and although he had determined to preserve strict silence in the
matter, early the following morning he
must take Zacche into his confidence.
They had scarcely finished speaking when
Hooper walked into the tailor shop and
hazarded a remark that was astonishingly
à propos.

'Hi, Mike, boy,' said he, 'let me be de
first to congratulate you upon de new

arrangement. Reginald getting on first-class—hi, yes! Patient man ride jackass —hi, yes! Don't you know that?'

'You is a funny man, though,' said Michael uneasily. 'Why don't you speak plain out? Give me you' meaning. How do I know what Reginald is doing?'

'That is it now,' exclaimed Hooper; 'that is de very thing. You don't know what Reginald is doing, and Reginald know that—hi, yes. I tell you so. Wake up, man, this is de time. Sleeping with you' eye open is just as dangerous as telling lie with you' eye shut, for you don't know what is happening in de meantime,' and he smiled.

'Well, sutt'nly,' said Zacche, 'Michael eye do open before this day, and he does know a thing or two. Howsomever, nothing can be done now. Sutt'nly we must watch and wait.'

It was therefore agreed that the business of securing evidence to condemn Reginald for ever should rest entirely in the hands of the three of them, and that, as Zacche suggested, they should watch and wait. Further, information obtained by one should be instantly communicated to the other two, and Zacche, the most innocent looking, was to be placed in every position of advantage.

Reginald and Mary were often together. Seated beside her on the small green lawn in front of the fort, Reginald would watch the sun set, and tell Mary, as he thought poetically, how beautiful was that love of his which would never set. Such love, he added was heavenly. Later, if the weather were fine, they would launch Michael's canoe, and Reginald would pull across the eastern harbour, still talking about that love of his that was so heavenly. And in the same hour Daddy and Mistriss Pengelly would, curiously enough, be seated in the cottage, the little kerosene light burning steadily and their old eyes sparkling with a happiness that could not be described.

No rain had fallen that afternoon and the evening was dry and fine. The moon rose early and with it a cool, sweet wind from the north. Reginald and Mary turned the church corner shortly after seven and walked swiftly and happily on in the direction of the Reservoir. They were followed at some distance by Zacche, Hooper and Michael, the latter carrying

a short, thick, pimento stick. When they
reached the gate that closes the path to
the Reservoir, the couple stopped, and
Reginald turned round twice, evidently
to see if they were being followed. And
had not Hooper, who was a few yards
ahead of Michael and Zacche, arrived
just then at the bend in the road,
Reginald must have seen him. Seeing
no one, however, Reginald opened the
gate, left the path and hurried with Mary
across a kind of field to a spot in the
wide shadow of a clump of bamboo trees.
Hooper, finding the gate open, called
cautiously to Zacche and Michael to
double up. The three then separated,
Michael keeping to the clear path which
led to the Reservoir, Zacche creeping
west close to a stone wall and Hooper

dodging his way to the clump of bamboo trees. Zacche, however, soon thinking that he was losing time in a wrong direction, got on his feet again and ran after Hooper, who now put up a hand to counsel silence. Slowly they approached the clump, Zacche stopping once or twice to pull a prickle from his heel. The breeze had freshened, and the bamboos creaked an accompaniment to the croaking of the toads and the piercing chirp of the water crickets, but loudest was the voice of the river to the right protesting at the stiffness of the stones. Presently there was a cry—a woman's cry —of agony and shame. It rose and fell and rose again before Hooper had time to spring to the spot. And then he found Mary sobbing and saw Reginald bending over her with his jacket in his hand.

'Hi, Reggie, you is here I see,' said Hooper, with a smile. 'Well now, this is what I call first-class; de only thing is, of course, you is a worthless fellow, and you deserve the biggest beating you ever have in your life—hi, yes, I am not joking.'

At the sound of Hooper's voice, both Reginald and Mary started, and Reginald, furious at his small success, and from the peculiar sting of Hooper's words, seized a bit of rock and flung it with all his strength at Hooper's head. Hooper dodged it, remarking quickly but coolly:

'And that is first-class too, being you mean to have a game with me. But I don't agree with you, Missa Reggie, as you will see.'

Then, before Reginald had time to comprehend his meaning, Hooper struck him a powerful blow full in the face, which sent Reginald sprawling to the ground. Mary, who had been trembling all over, now commenced to shriek, and it was this shrieking that summoned Michael to the scene. Zacche, too, came up panting about this time. He had fallen into a muddy hog hole, and was unable, therefore, to put in an earlier appearance. Quickly recovering his breath, he first addressed Mary to comfort her.

'Well, sutt'nly, my dear,' said he, putting his arms tenderly round her, 'you have had a fright — whichen is what some female really want; but no damage, no damage, so wipe you' eyes. Sutt'nly we is here now to protect you.'

Negro Nobodies

Michael, speechless with rage, lifted his stick to beat the life out of Reginald, but Hooper held his arm.

'You going put you'self in a perspiration for nothing, man,' he reasoned; 'hi, yes! I tell you so. Now, this is it, we three will take charge of Missa Reginald, and Missa Reginald, of course, can take charge of us, and we is going to de cottage now—hi, yes (turning to Reginald, still furious, but who saw, from the arrival of Michael and Zacche, that fighting was useless), hi, yes, man, and you is going to tell Missa Daddy all about de angel them from heaven who are with you now, whichen is we. Hi, yes, of course.'

'Well, sutt'nly,' said Zacche, who had succeeded in quieting Mary, 'sutt'nly de

night is dark and we are far from home—
whichen that may not exactly be de case,
but it's a line from de hymn book all de
same—nevertheless I propose we right
about face and out of this place sharp,
sharp. Only, sutt'nly,' pointing, with his
muddy finger, to a certain spot, 'there is
a small hog hole over there, whichen
you must mind.'

Michael then took Mary's hand, and
Zacche and Hooper, getting on either
side of Reginald, the party started to
walk across the field. Before they had
proceeded many yards, however, Reginald
suddenly stooped and caught Zacche by
the legs, lifting and throwing him against
Hooper, who fell also. Reginald then
bolted in the opposite direction and was
soon out of sight.

Negro Nobodies

'Sutt'nly,' said Zacche, rising and wiping his mouth, 'that man is hell.'

'Well, yes,' assented Hooper, 'but we is hell also, de only thing is we give him a chance to make his escape.'

'Ah,' sobbed Mary, 'don't disturb him, don't disturb him. Oh, have pity on me, pity me and leave him. . . . He promised to take me for a walk to this said place that was indeed lovely, and I would be so happy with him there, he said. Did I doubt him? Oh, could I doubt him? Was he not really a handsome man? Oh, what a thing is love, for now I know it can deceive you. . . . Then, suddenly, he held me, he kissed me, he—oh, God, what shall I do? For I am indeed ruined. It must be so. I am lost, lost, lost. Oh, Michael, Michael, what am I to tell father?'

The Overseas Library

'Well, don't distress you'self,' said
Zacche kindly, 'no damage, no damage,
my dear—whichen we all hope. Sutt'nly
I watch him and come to de conclusion
that he was not to be trusted. We
watched him this very evening and made
an arrangement—whichen it has come to
pass that we was right and de fellow get
a surprise. Sutt'nly life is a funny thing,
being you don't know what to expect
next, and de cleverest man is de man who
know that God Almighty put his sense
and his two eye them in his head for
more purpose than one.'

On their way to the cottage they met
Daddy returning from a visit to Mother
Bet. The old man seemed lost in
thought, and, when he heard Mary's
half-stifled sobs, he put his hand to his

head and stared at them as if he had lost his senses. The truth is, Daddy had that night learnt for the first time of the true character of Reginald Pengelly, and was still puzzling over the course of action he should pursue when the party approached. Then Mary's sobs and the expressions on the faces of her companions so rudely confirmed his worst suspicions, that he suffered a terrible shock. Indeed he would have fallen had not Hooper supported him. And it was not until some minutes afterwards, when he appeared to be calmer, that Zacche, with great tact and delicacy, ventured to give him an idea of what had happened.

About twelve o'clock that night, when the town was sound asleep, and the moon, shining in a cloudless sky, spread a soft, clear light, like a silken sheet, upon the land; while the wind blew gently upon the trees, and Nature herself seemed in a beautiful dream, there wandered, ghostlike, upon Titchfield Hill, two figures. The one, sighing, was Mistriss Pengelly. The other I need not name.

THE END

Colston & Coy. Limited, Printers, Edinburgh.